ALS

Coming Soon
The Red Rose

Short Story
Work-Crush Balance

Cedar Creek
Christmas at Cedar Creek
Snowstorm at Cedar Creek
Sunlight on Cedar Creek

Pine Harbor
Allison's Pine Harbor Summer
Evelyn's Pine Harbor Autumn
Lydia's Pine Harbor Christmas

Holiday House
The Christmas Cabin
The Winter Lodge
The Lighthouse
The Christmas Castle
The Beach House
The Christmas Tree Inn

The Holiday Hideaway

Highland Passage
Highland Passage
Knight Errant
Lost Bride

Highland Soldiers
The Enemy
The Betrayal
The Return
The Wanderer

Highland Vow

American Hearts
Secret Hearts
Runaway Hearts
Forbidden Hearts

For more information, visit jljarvis.com.

Get monthly book news at news.jljarvis.com.

THE WINTER LODGE

THE WINTER LODGE

A HOLIDAY HOUSE NOVEL

J.L. JARVIS

BOOKBINDER PRESS

THE WINTER LODGE
A Holiday House Novel

Published by Bookbinder Press
bookbinderpress.com

ISBN 978-1-942767-06-0 (paperback)
ISBN 978-1-942767-05-3 (ebook)

He thought it a very degrading alliance; and Lady Russell, though with more tempered and pardonable pride, received it as a most unfortunate one.

—Jane Austen, *Persuasion*

ONE

"There are worse things in life than getting laid off," Piper Harriman said to herself. "There are better things too, like *not* getting laid off."

She gripped the wheel and headed up I-95 out of Boston. Her all-wheel-drive car was packed with boxes and trash bags full of clothes still on the hangers. She'd left her sparse furnishings behind for the next occupant of her Allston-Brighton apartment.

So, this was it—her whole life in a hatchback. This was her takeaway from four years of college and four years as an accountant for a small tech startup. Her company had been bought out, and she was kicked to the curb with a glowing letter of recommendation. Her cashed-out 401K might get her through the next six months, if she was lucky.

Her phone rang, interrupting the current song on

her "Laid Off and Driving Home to Live in My Parents' Basement" playlist. "Hi. I'm driving. Yes, Dad, I'm using a hands-free device." She shook her head, smiling. "I'll be fine. I'll see you in about four hours."

Her smile turned to a curious frown. "I won't? Oh, okay."

It wasn't exactly okay. She'd wanted to go home and feel the comfort of having family around. It was a small family, just her father and stepmother. Their flight to Florida had been cancelled, so they were put on an earlier flight. They'd be gone by the time she got there.

She sighed. "No, I can manage. Don't worry. I'm sorry, what? Oh." They'd rented the house. "So where will I stay?" Before her dad answered, she nodded. Their holiday rental next door.

The call was dropped, which was fine. It gave her time to reason out why they were renting their large coastal home instead of the small cottage next door, which they'd always called "The Lodge." The name was a little pretentious for a small holiday rental, but it had been The Lodge for as long as she could remember, so why tamper with tradition? During high school, they'd winterized it. From then on, they'd jokingly called it "The Winter Lodge," even though most of their rental business was during the summer season. But they'd finished the remodel in winter, so The Winter Lodge stuck.

That was also when the whole Juan Calderon thing happened. It didn't take long for those memories to come uninvited to the front of her mind.

HIS FATHER WAS WORKING on the cabin, with Juan's help. Juan and Piper went to the same school, so she'd seen him around. But there was something about his tall, sinewy body in work boots and a tool belt that caught her attention.

One day, some friends dropped her off at home after staying late at school. Juan was getting something from the truck as she walked down the driveway.

She said, "Hi."

"Hi."

She pointed to the Calderon Construction sign on the side of the truck. "That's your father?"

"Yeah."

Piper said, "So you work for him?"

He nodded. "Except during baseball season."

She nodded back and looked into his eyes. That was when it started. That one simple encounter changed everything. From then on, there was an unspoken awareness, a charge in the air between them.

"Juan!" his father called out from the front door of the lodge.

Juan's eyes shone as he smiled. Looking back, she realized that the smile she returned was more of a zombified stare. Juan's father waited in the doorway with a stern look on his face.

Piper said, "I'd better let you get back to work."

"Yeah." He looked away, grabbed a sheet of drywall from the bed of the pickup, and carried it into the lodge.

Piper couldn't help but watch him. He was all strong arms and shoulders. When her eyes drifted down to the blue jeans and tool belt, something in the periphery caught her attention. Juan's father. He'd watched her watch Juan, and he didn't look too pleased about it. But Juan was so hot, with his nearly black hair and those deep, brooding brown eyes. How could any girl be expected not to notice?

Piper turned away as though nothing had happened, then tightened her grip on her backpack straps and went into the house.

A BLACK SPORTS car passed by a little too closely and forced Piper back to the present, in high-alert mode. It proceeded to weave in and out of traffic until it was safely away—safely for her, anyway. She calmed down and put the cruise control back on.

Back to Juan Calderon. Piper rubbed her forehead. Nearly eight years ago, in the summer after high school graduation, they had sat on a secluded stretch of coastline on a warm August night with a cool ocean breeze. Before long, their two bodies were a tangle of passion and promises. Two kids in love, they were going to get married.

Until the next day, when her father said no. She was too young, and Juan was not a suitable match. He didn't come from money, wasn't going to college, and there was that thing her father never said because he was too politically correct to say such things out loud. Maybe it wasn't about Juan's ethnicity. Maybe it was because of their disparate tax brackets and social circles. Whatever it was, this marriage was not going to happen if her father had anything to say about it.

And he did. If she married Juan, her father wouldn't pay for college. Could Juan Calderon put her through school? No? Well then, she should wait four years. Reluctantly, she agreed.

Juan didn't take it well when she told him. It

might have been easier if he'd argued or accused her of being too weak to stand up to her father—or if he'd just yelled. Something. He'd have been right, no matter what.

But instead, he said nothing. He never begged her to stay or told her that he'd miss her. He simply accepted her choice with a clenched jaw and a dark, faraway look in his eyes. Then he gave her a kiss that would ruin all kisses to come after. She should have known it then, but it wasn't until the next morning, when she drove off to college and he hadn't come to say goodbye, that she realized the kiss had been his farewell forever.

THE PHONE RANG. It was her father again. They'd made it to the airport. All checked in and ready to board. Oh, by the way, did she remember Juan Calderon?

Could he even ask that without knowing the answer? Was the memory of Juan not seared into the healed-over break in her heart? If having her heart skip a beat at the mention of his name eight years later constituted remembering him, well then, yes. Yes, she did.

"Uh, yeah, why? Really? He's rented the house?

Our house? No, no, that's... fine. Yes, really."

Not really.

"Okay, go fight the good fight for your overhead bin. Have a good trip. Love you. Bye."

Eight years. The mere thought of seeing him made her tachycardic—which meant nothing except that she had a good memory. She couldn't still be "in love" because that was the stuff of pathetic romantics, which she was not. In the eight years since Juan, she'd never felt anything close to that feeling, nor would she. Those feelings were best left in the formative years, in that window of time between unbridled love and fathomable regret. She'd grown past all of that because she was grown up.

Adulthood was simply a matter of narrowing one's expectations to achievable levels that may or may not involve love. Relationships never ended. The text messages just stopped. Then the memories were stashed like dollar-store bins in a closet. Piper's memory bins were labeled with four Ws: Why? Why not? Whatever! And WTF was that? And they were never heard from again.

Now, Juan was going to be her neighbor. As such, there was a good chance she would see him at some point. More than once, even. Possibly daily. At such times, she would be expected *not* to look at him just like she had *not* looked at him when his father was watching. Even so, she was an adult. Naturally, it might be a little uncomfortable at first. But so were tampons, and she'd grown used to them.

Hmm. Piper shook her head and made a mental note—no more vaginal analogies.

Back to Juan. Before long, it would just be the occasional passing hello wave, and life would go on. There was no need to blow this thing out of proportion.

SHE PULLED INTO THE DRIVEWAY. The house hadn't changed much, except for the pickup truck parked there. She wanted to believe it belonged to a worker preparing the house for rental. But given the way Piper's luck had been running lately, she'd bet her severance package it was Juan's. So, proceeding with caution, she pulled past the pickup bearing a Calderon Construction sign on the side, and she parked in the small patch of driveway by the lodge.

For a moment, she sat breathing deeply. *Okay.* She smoothed back her fiery curls, grabbed the overnight bag with her essentials, got out of her car, and walked to the lodge with a purpose—that purpose being to make it inside without seeing Juan.

She just wasn't ready. Maybe after a shower, a blow dry, a complete makeup overhaul, and a full glass of wine, she'd consider it. Until then, it was long strides, a quick grab for the key hiding over the doorframe, and then she was in. Door closed. *Phew!*

As she leaned on the inside of the front door, a car door slammed outside, and an engine started up. She peeked through a crack in the blinds. She wasn't proud of the move, but she did it. Dusk had settled in, making it hard to see Juan clearly, but it was his truck. He backed out of the driveway and was gone. Piper fired up the potbelly stove for some heat and headed out to the car, hurrying to unload it before he came back.

Saving the serious unpacking for tomorrow, she poured a glass of wine and sat down by the window to look at the view. The Winter Lodge sat beside the main house on a hill overlooking the horseshoe-shaped harbor. Most boats were in storage for the winter, leaving the snow-dusted harbor looking stark except for a few fishing boats that defied winter. The holiday lights, combined with the usual harbor lights, shone like thick shimmering ribbons of color that reached for the horizon and faded from view.

Piper shivered and moved to an overstuffed chair by the fire, where she rested her legs on an old wooden trunk. Arranging a throw blanket over her legs, she leaned back and stared at the flickering flames. This would be her home. For a while, anyway. Perhaps staying here had worked out for the best. The lodge was actually larger than her Boston apartment, with wide-plank oak floors and a cozy bedroom off to the side of the house. The kitchen was open to the living room, which was lined with tall windows covered by cream-colored linen curtains.

It was comfortable and warm, but she still felt adrift with no job and no family around—and worst of all, with no plan. She'd always set goals and worked hard because if you did that, you'd succeed. And it had worked. She'd been rolling along, working hard, getting rewarded for her efforts. Until now. Now she had nothing. No job, no family—at least not nearby—and no place to go. This was not how her life was supposed to work out.

Oh—and she'd left out *alone*. Of course, that wasn't new, but she had all this time to reflect on it. She'd trained herself fairly well to suppress such thoughts. Anymore, they only surfaced after a date or a breakup. She would say good night and try not to sigh with relief until well out of earshot. Sometimes an evening went well enough to end with a kiss, only to have the prince turn into a frog when the touch of his lips rendered nothing—no spark, no racing pulse, no chemistry.

HER FIRST KISS with Juan was electric. They'd been friends at first. He appeared at her side in the lunch line one day. After that, it was daily. It just grew from there. There were no grand declarations or even discussions of what their relationship was or was going to be. They just knew.

They both had a study hall together. One day, Piper had to cram for a chemistry quiz. Juan had been watching her over a library table with a mischievous look in his eyes. She could feel his deep gaze, and she couldn't help but smile, which only made everything worse—well, worse as it related to her chemistry quiz, but better in regard to her life. But the quiz was the next period, and she didn't feel close to ready.

Juan leaned forward and urgently whispered, "Piper, come here. I need to show you something." He held her gaze with those dark eyes of his. Oh, that feeling she'd get! The whole world disappeared when he looked in her eyes. No one had ever made her feel that way before or since, and with only a look.

He got up, and she followed him down the row between two tall shelves. He pointed to a book halfway down the row and just above eye level. She frowned and squinted as she read the title and tried to figure out why he'd felt the need to show her this particular book at this particular time. Whatever the title was, she would never remember, because as she lifted her chin to decipher the faded gold letters on the worn fabric volume, he put his hand on her cheek and bent down to kiss her. That kiss didn't end until the bell rang minutes later, and she had to hurry to chemistry class to make it in time.

SHE THOUGHT OF THAT KISS, and so many others, and the way his hand brushed softly against hers as they went their separate ways to class. And she wondered. What would have happened if she'd given up college and stayed here with Juan?

At the time, she'd been too unsure of herself, so she'd trusted the adults in her life when they told her that she was too young to really be in love, let alone to get married. Whatever this was, it could wait until after college. She'd believed their insistence that she couldn't know what love really was at eighteen. They were older and wiser. What did she know? She just thought it was love.

But now, she was older and knew it had been love.

TWO

Piper woke the next morning with an adrenaline hangover. The work stress was gone, but in a matter of days, she'd lost her job, packed up her apartment, and made the drive home. Now, her calendar was clear for the day—and indefinitely—and she wasn't quite sure what to do with herself after coffee.

As she lifted the lid on the French press coffee maker, a truck door closed outside. *Juan's truck?* She looked up, her hand slipped, and all of her hopes and dreams—for coffee, anyway—shattered all over the floor. Choosing to ignore how symbolic this was of her life, she swept up the pieces and formed a new plan.

On her way to work every day, she used to look inside the coffee shop windows and envy the people who sat there, all relaxed and in charge of their time.

Now, she could be one of those people. She showered and got dressed but didn't bother with makeup because she didn't have to. She had entered the ranks of the nonworking free.

She slid into a booth at the Dockside Diner. After exchanging small talk with the server, an old classmate from high school, Piper opened the local newspaper and lost herself in it. Some things hadn't changed. The town hummed with the usual small-town issues and events. The library was having its annual used-book sale. After some controversy about paving over part of the beauty that drew tourists to town, the town board voted to add a new parking lot to accommodate seasonal visitors who clogged downtown streets and driveways. In other news, people had married, while others had died, among them her old English teacher. She was seized with a swell of emotion. That was part of the deal. Things ended—not only jobs, but people's lives, people's loves. They were never meant to last forever.

"Piper?"

She looked up, startled, and stared blankly. "Juan?" Coming to her senses, she smiled. "Hello." Her hand twitched in an impulse to reach out and shake his hand, but touching him suddenly seemed like too much. She didn't trust her reaction, so she stopped and just stared.

"How are you?" he asked.

His boyish, Latin good looks had made an impressive transition to manhood. He'd always had deep-brown eyes and brilliant white teeth, but his now beard-stubbled jaw had squared out a bit, as had his shoulders. He still had the same gaze that could render her brainless and slack-jawed if she wasn't prepared—and she wasn't.

When she realized it was her turn to talk and not gape, she said, "Fine."

He nodded, his eyes locked on hers. His lips parted as if he might say something. *I still love you.* No, that was what she might say if she weren't careful.

A cheery voice interrupted, "Piper! Hello! What brings you back to town?"

Piper forced a smile. "Tiffany."

There was no mistaking Tiffany Tucker, even with all her sable hair cropped to a smart pixie cut that set off her electric-blue, contact-lens-tinted eyes. Her poor skirt barely reached the legs it was intended to cover, leaving a gap between it and her thigh-high boots. She looked great, and that just wasn't fair. For Piper, Tiffany would always be the same high-school cheerleader in sneakers who could torment lesser mortals with a sweep of her eyes as she turned away with a smirk.

Back in high school, when word had gotten around that Piper and Juan were together, Tiffany and her friends shoved crumbled taco chips and squeezed Mexican hot sauce through the vents in Piper's locker. Piper wasn't one to hold a grudge, but it was hard to forget something like that. She'd ditched her next class to clean it all up before Juan could see it. That would only have doubled Tiffany's glee.

Tiffany tilted her head with a questioning look, waiting for her answer.

And what was the question? Piper squinted for a moment. Ah, yes, what had brought her back to town. "I've come back because this is my hometown."

"Oh, how nice. How long are you here for?"

Piper looked frankly at her. "I don't know."

Tiffany put on an award-winning smile. "Well, take care."

Juan raised his eyes from the point on the table they'd been fixed on. Tiffany hooked her arm into his and said, "Shall we?"

His eyes darted from Tiffany to Piper. "Good to see you, Piper."

"You too."

While the pair went to the back of the diner and sat in a booth, Piper marveled at how much awkwardness could be packed into one three-second look. Barring a more precise measure, she went with "a lot."

Now that her appetite had been ruined, Piper's breakfast arrived. She ate what she could and left half on her plate. She couldn't see Juan and Tiffany without swiveling her head to the back of the diner, so she relied on her peripheral vision to determine when the coast was clear, and she made a direct line for the cash register. As she waited for her card to process, Tiffany's giggle drew near. Someone greeted Juan, and they chatted. Pretending not to notice any of what went on behind her, Piper tapped her fingers against her thigh while the cashier made small talk with another customer.

"It's done," Piper said to the cashier as she pointed to the machine. When the cashier continued her chat, Piper thought about climbing over the counter but couldn't decide whether to grab her card from the machine or grab the cashier's polyester uniform lapel. Just as she'd decided upon the lapel, the cashier abstractedly pulled out the card and held the receipt and card in Piper's direction. Piper scribbled her signature. With a quick "thanks," she made her escape. The sound of the door closing behind her was drowned out by her heart, which was hammering out its own rendition of the Anvil Chorus.

HOME AGAIN AFTER an hour-long errand run,
Piper set down a bag of groceries. Staying busy was
the key, she'd decided. She tackled the kitchen, then
cleaned the lodge, which was already spotless from
the weekly house cleanings her parents paid for to
keep the lodge ready for rental. She stared at the sofa
cushions and rearranged them one more time. *Okay,
done.* Maybe she'd go for a walk.

Well-dressed for cold weather, she ventured
outside and down to the harbor, where a boardwalk
skirted the waterfront. There she sat on a bench and
listened first to her thoughts, but those drifted away as
the water lapped against the moored boats with a
rhythmic insistence that some things had not changed
since she'd lived here. The ocean still met the shore that
swept up to the hill where the pine trees reached up to
the sky and the sun shone between the branches. This
comforted her. It somehow implied a promise that she
would fall back into its rhythm, for she was part of it all.

"I remember how you used to like coming here."

Piper flinched and looked up to find Juan
standing before her, backlit by the sun like a Byzan-
tine icon with a gold-leaf halo.

"Yeah. Still do, apparently."

They exchanged smiles. His was evasive, while hers sent her reeling back through time to the age of thirteen—not her best year. She turned back and gazed at the ocean, embarrassed by the heat in her cheeks that promised an adolescent-scale blush would soon follow.

He shifted his weight and followed her gaze to the water. "I wanted to talk to you sooner."

She smiled and shrugged. "I just got here last night."

His lips spread into that smile she'd always loved. It went from his even white teeth and full lips to the small lines that spread from the outside corners of his eyes. "I mean last night, when I saw your car. But I didn't want to intrude."

She looked up with an eye-rolling smirk that drew a laugh.

He shook his head. "Same old Piper."

She lifted her eyes and felt that same old Piper feeling for him.

He combed his fingers through his thick shock of straight black hair. "Look, when I rented the house, I didn't know you'd be living next door. Your parents never mentioned it."

Piper tried not to frown. "They didn't know. It was kind of a spontaneous thing." She averted her eyes, but then had to look back, unable to help herself. She blamed pheromones.

He squinted, but then nodded as though she'd made perfect sense. "Well, anyway, I just wanted to say that the past is the past. We've grown up and, well, we're going to be next-door neighbors. I don't want it to be uncomfortable. You know?"

Too late for that. "Yeah." She smiled as if she meant it and looked into his eyes, which was a mistake. A momentary jolt of the old longing caught her off guard. She at least managed to make her voice sound cheerful. "Look at us, all grown up."

Their nervous laughter faded as his eyes lingered on hers. Then his mood shifted abruptly. "Oh, and I wanted to tell you there's no washer and dryer in the lodge, so you're welcome to use mine. Yours, actually —or your parents'—you know what I mean."

"Thanks. I hadn't thought that far ahead, to tell you the truth."

"Well, I remembered how your parents let me use their laundry room when I stayed in the lodge."

"You stayed there?"

"Oh, well, it was just for a couple of months, after my dad died. Thanks for the card, by the way."

Piper's brow furrowed. "At the time, I thought coming back for the funeral might not be the best idea, but... I don't know." A sudden swell of emotion rose from her chest. "I was so sorry to hear it, and I felt like I ought to do something. You know?"

For a moment, she looked into his eyes, and even now, after all the years that had passed, the connection was there. Speaking about the past and the people they'd loved brought it close to the surface. It only lasted a moment, and then it was gone, leaving Piper and Juan and the silence between them.

He glanced toward the sea. "Anyway, to answer your question, the house sold more quickly than I expected, so I had to move out."

Piper nodded and tried to look pleasant, but it saddened her to think that he'd sold the home he'd grown up in. "And now?"

He looked confused for a moment. "Oh, now? Well, I'm renting your house while I'm building my own."

"Oh? Where?"

"I lucked into some waterfront property, so I'm building on it."

Piper's eyebrows lifted involuntarily. Waterfront property was prime real estate. That was some kind of luck.

Juan shrugged. "Anyway, if you need to do laundry, the key's in the same place your parents always leave it—under the flowerpot on the left."

She nodded. "Because who would ever think to look there?"

They chuckled together, and the glimpse of normalcy between them made her heart ache for what she'd given up years ago. The fact that she'd done this to herself made it worse. After all, what right did she have to feel anything for him?

Juan took a breath as though he was going to say something, but a staccato laugh rang out from down the walkway.

"Wow, look at you two. Just like old times." Avery Schmidt's straight brown hair brushed the collar of her knee-length, camel-colored wool coat as she walked toward them, grinning. Juan took a step back as though this was his cue to escape. Piper stood to give Avery a hug.

"I heard you'd come home."

"Yeah." Piper nodded with a self-deprecating smirk.

Avery's forehead creased as she opened her mouth, no doubt to ask why. Thankfully, Avery closed her mouth and nodded instead.

Piper's eyes flitted toward Juan, who looked just as curious, but he had the good sense not to ask.

Well, why not get it out in the open? "I, uh, well, the company I worked for was sold, and the new owners had their own accountants. So... they gave me a severance package and a cardboard box to pack up the shards of my career. And here I am."

With a sad sigh, Avery said, "Sorry, Pipes."

No one else called her that, and she smiled to hear it again.

"That explains why you went quiet online."

"Yeah, I wasn't quite ready to shout it from the rooftops or social media."

Juan said, "Sorry to hear that."

"Thanks." Despite everything they'd been through, he was still being kind. She almost wished he'd do something to help her hate him. Although, breakfast with Tiffany at the diner was a pretty good start. *Still, it was better than breakfast at Tiffany's— not the film—which would mean... never mind.*

Avery looked from Juan to Piper. "So... when Betsy at the diner said she'd seen you, I figured you couldn't have gone far."

Piper raised her eyebrows. "And here I am."

Avery glanced at her watch. "Oh, man. I'm due back at the office. I'll call you!"

As Avery rushed off, Piper said. "She hasn't changed."

"No."

They both watched her round the corner. Piper turned back to Juan. "Well, I'd better let you get on with your day."

Juan wasted no time in responding. "Yeah. Look, I'll see you around." He hesitated.

Had he leaned closer? It was as if he'd decided to give her a hug but changed his mind. Abruptly, he turned and walked away. Piper took a deep breath and let it out slowly. She'd seen him, they'd talked, and both would live to face another day. Now all she had to do was get over him.

She returned to her car and sank into the seat. He didn't hate her, at least not outwardly. So now she could get on with her new life back home. She took another deep breath. It was time to move on to more practical matters, like a new coffee maker. That would make everything better. She started the car and was off for a day of retail therapy on an unemployed budget.

JUAN PULLED onto the road that ran through the center of town and headed for the construction site where his new home would be. A cold wind blew in off the ocean. After a quick inspection of the progress on the house's interior, he pulled his knit cap over his ears and shoved his hands into his pockets and made his way to a narrow foot path that followed the shoreline. With one glance back at his house, he took off at a run.

He'd done it—picked the scab off an old wound that had never fully healed. He'd spoken with Piper, his new next-door neighbor. It had not been as uncomfortable as he'd expected, only painful. Before he saw her, he'd been sure he was over her, for the most part, and yet it astonished him how everything came back with such clarity.

It was that summer again, with the cool ocean breeze at his back as he stood in the driveway alone. Her father had said no. They could not be together. It could have been because he was Hispanic or because he didn't come from money. It was probably both, but he would never know for sure. All he would know was the ache in his heart as Piper drove off to college and left him behind.

It was no wonder their moment of parting had defined everything he'd done with his life ever since. He'd stood in that driveway and vowed he would never let anyone make him feel like that again.

He went to work for his father, which had always been the plan. But now he was fueled by an insatiable drive to achieve. He worked in the daytime and went to college online in the evenings, taking as many classes as he could afford each semester. After long days of manual labor, he went home and studied until late in the night. It took him seven years, but he did it. He finished college with a finance degree.

Along the way, he'd invested in the stock market and traded online. He'd kept his father's construction company for sentimental reasons. It was his investing that provided the bulk of his financial security. His coffers were full, but his heart was still empty.

What bothered him the most about seeing her again was the way his heart ached to open up to her. The same heart that was quick to remember the pain seemed all too eager for more. For years, his deepest desire had been to hate her. Somewhere in the back of his mind, as he'd studied and prospered, he'd bitterly hoped for the chance to rub her nose in his bank statement. What better time could there be than now? She'd lost her job. She'd moved home because she'd had to. She was alone and as vulnerable as she'd ever been. With their fortunes reversed, he could hurt her, perhaps not as much as she'd once hurt him, but enough.

But he couldn't. He couldn't do it because all he could think of was holding her and...

Juan stopped running and bent down to lean on his knees while he caught his breath. That was enough running—and thinking and feeling—for now.

PIPER LEFT the last bite of her microwaved frozen dinner behind and answered the door.

Before the door was fully open, Avery said, "First of all, you really ought to check your social media more often. I messaged you I was coming. I'd have called too, but I don't have your cell number. Second, I'm sorry." She held out a six pack of craft beer and winced. "Peace offering?"

Piper stepped back and waved her arm to invite her friend inside. "For what?"

Avery sighed. "I thought I was rescuing you from an awkward encounter, but I realized too late that I'd barged in on something."

"You didn't barge in. Relax." Piper took the beer into the kitchen. "Would you like one?"

Avery's eyes crinkled as she smiled. "I thought you'd never ask."

They sat down on the sofa in front of the wall of windows that overlooked the harbor. The last ribbon of sunset was shining over the water.

Avery hugged a throw pillow and took a sip of her beer. "So, how was it?" When Piper frowned as if she didn't understand, Avery said, "Seeing Juan."

Piper shook her head and exhaled. "It's been eight years."

"I'm not asking how long it's been. I'm asking

how it was seeing him. Do you still have feelings for him?"

Piper shook her head. Spying Avery's empty bottle, she got up and took it. "Be right back," she said without answering the question.

They spent the rest of the evening catching up on the local news. Piper had surmised, from social media posts over the years, that Juan had done well with his business. Not that he would have bragged about it. It was only apparent between the lines of his posts and confirmed by what others had posted. He was often pictured in local newspaper coverage of charity fund-raising events alongside the same people who had snubbed him in high school.

Avery stretched out her legs and took a swig from her beer. "He's still single."

That was a heck of a way to fill a lull in the conversation. Piper thought about pretending she didn't know whom Avery was talking about, but Avery's knowing look made it clear her attempts would be futile.

Piper upended her bottle and finished her beer. "That ship sailed a long time ago."

"Ships can come back into port."

Piper's face wrinkled up.

Avery's eyes widened. "That might not have

come out right. I didn't mean literally. Well, not exactly literally, but, you know, maybe sort of..."

Piper held up her palm. "Stop. There's no saving it." They both laughed as Piper reached for Avery's empty beer bottle. "Another?"

"No, thanks. I've got an early meeting tomorrow." On her way to the door, Avery said, "Some of us are going sledding on Saturday. Want to join us?"

"Sure. I could use the exercise." And something to do besides watch people drive off to work every morning.

"Good. I'll text you. Oh, give me your number." With their numbers exchanged, Avery left for home.

Piper waved as Avery pulled out of the driveway, then she noticed a light in the window of the main house. Juan was home. And what business was that of hers?

THREE

It was only a matter of time before laundry had to be done. During the last few days, Piper had finished unpacking, she'd shopped for food and essentials, she'd looked for jobs, and she'd cleaned the lodge. Again. There was no putting it off any longer. She gathered up her clothes and headed for home—or rather, Juan's home. His truck had been gone for a half hour, so the coast was clear.

Laundry gave her time to think. Lately, that hadn't been a good thing. She loaded the washer and started to head for the lodge, but instead, she took a quick detour to revisit childhood memories with a walk through the house she'd grown up in.

It didn't feel quite right to go wandering upstairs and down the hall. *Maybe because it isn't right*, she reminded herself. It might still look like her home, but it was Juan's home for now. Still, she couldn't help herself. She hadn't been home in so long. She was drawn to the warmth of her childhood memories. Juan was there too, in those memories.

She turned the knob to her bedroom, which hadn't changed since she'd last left it. It was a time capsule of her youth, in which she half expected the ghost of high school past to appear in a mist, offering a glimpse of her eighteen-year-old self in action.

She took in a quick breath. Had Juan come in here? Why not? He had rented the place and had every right to. But she'd found the door closed. He had probably looked once and shut it in horror to seal off any reminder of their time together.

Piper heaved a sigh. *That's enough! Moving on.* She closed the door and went back to the lodge to wait for her laundry to dry.

After lunch, she was back, gathering her laundry from the dryer, when she heard Juan's truck pull into the driveway. No worries. They were on amiable footing. She'd say hello and be on her way. This was actually good. The more they saw one another, the more normal it would feel.

She lifted her overflowing basket of laundry and headed for the door, trying to time it so she'd pass him before he reached the door. If need be, she'd make use of the basket in her arms as an excuse not to linger and chat. She backed out of the door and let it swing shut. Turning, she saw him as he closed his truck door.

"Hello." She smiled.

He waved and said, "Hi." And she was off.

When she'd scurried halfway across the driveway, he called out to her, "You dropped something."

Piper shut her eyes, took in a sharp breath, and whispered, "No." What was it? Bra? Thong? Favorite T-shirt with pit stains? She turned around and saw something wadded in his hand, but she couldn't tell what it was. Piper squared her shoulders and walked toward him with her best simulation of dignity. She reached out her hand, and he put something in it.

She looked down. "Oh." *Thank God. A dishcloth.*

She lifted her eyes and tried to ignore the slight upturned corner of his mouth and the barest bit of a glint in his eyes. His eyes narrowed. "What?"

She tightened the dishcloth in her hand and smiled. "Nothing. Just thank you." Quickly, before he could read any more into her expression, she turned and walked what now seemed like a mile to her door.

SHE WAS STILL RECOVERING from the laundry incident, which was only an incident in her poor self-conscious mind. Evidently, all of her inter-actions with Juan were going to be over-imagined, dissected, and reassembled into some sort of post-adolescent fret fest for those moments when life got too comfortable. Once she accepted that as the norm, she'd be fine. So when someone knocked on the door, she shrugged helplessly. *Here we go again.*

She swung open the door. "What did I forget this time?"

But it wasn't Juan standing there. A tall thirty-ish blond guy stood before her, casually but expensively dressed.

"Nothing yet." He smiled as if he'd perfected the art, and he may have come close.

Piper couldn't take her gaze off of his icy-blue eyes. This was not entirely her fault, since they were fixed firmly on hers. And he was grinning. Broadly. A cartoon sparkle would not have surprised her. "I'm sorry. I thought you were someone else."

It was his turn to speak, and the fact that it took him a moment made her uneasy. She smiled, mainly because he had started it.

"Your groundskeeper sent me over here."

"My what?" Piper looked past the visitor to the driveway, where Juan was carrying an armload of wood into the house. Several possible responses ran through Piper's mind, but she settled on a simple, "Oh, no. He lives there."

"But Hadley..."

"Is renting it to him while he's away." She couldn't help eyeing him with a quizzical look. He knew her father? What else did he know?

"Oh, he must be in Florida. Well, then, never mind." He glanced over his shoulder toward the main house and laughed.

As attractive as he was, upper-crust blonds from old money were not Piper's thing, so she was ready to move on with her day. "Is there something I can help you with?"

He turned his laser eyes back on her. "Yes. Sorry. I'm Grayson Endicott, a golf buddy of Hadley's."

At least something made sense. Piper now felt a bit more at ease.

"And you must be Piper."

She smiled. "I am. And, yes, he's in Florida."

"He's mentioned you several times." He leaned toward her. "I think he thought we'd make a good pair."

Piper wrinkled her forehead in confusion. "Did he?"

The smile that came next, with those perfect white teeth and pale-blue eyes, was so winning and

yet looked well-practiced—to the point of perfection
—that Piper imagined few ladies resisted its charms.
She was managing, but just barely.

"I'd love to see Pine Harbor from your point of
view. When are you free?"

If he hadn't been so smooth, Piper might not have
been so reluctant, but there was something about his
well-mannered poise that made her hesitate. It
shouldn't have, she supposed. After all, he'd come
recommended by her own father. But she couldn't
shake her instinctive resistance.

She smiled graciously. "It's so kind of you to
follow through with my father's suggestion. I'm sure
he'll appreciate that. But I've got a lot on my plate at
the moment."

Unfazed, he pulled a business card from his
pocket. "If your schedule opens up, here's where you
can reach me."

Piper studied the card. "The Endicott Group.
And you're..."

"Grayson Endicott. Founder, CEO." He
shrugged with an endearing, if false, modesty.

"Well, it was nice to meet you, Grayson." She
extended her hand, and he shook it.

"Nice to meet you, Piper."

She watched Grayson Endicott head for his shiny

black foreign sports car, and she closed her door. That she immediately went to the window to peer out as he drove off spoke volumes more than she cared to admit. She couldn't have explained why she'd done it. He wasn't her type. Not exactly. Although, to be honest, a guy as good-looking as that could be pretty much anyone's type, so why not? A girl had a right to window shop once in a while. And here she was at a window.

Perhaps one strike against him was that her father had sent him. Grayson was the sort of man he approved of for her—a guy dripping with wealth who said all the right things, whether he meant them or not. Those were her father's criteria—not hers. She felt fairly sure that if her father adored him, he'd be all wrong for her. So, really, she had just saved them both wasted time.

PIPER WINCED from the glare of the sun on the snow as she opened the hatch of her car and muttered to Avery, "I don't know why I let you talk me into this." But she knew why, or at least how. They'd been having a couple of Friday-night drinks, and Piper's defenses were down. So here she was, bright and early on a Saturday morning, pulling

Avery's wooden toboggan and snow tube out of the back of her car.

"It's going to be fun!" Avery chirped, showing no sign of the late hour at which they'd left the Harbor House Bar on the previous night. Piper, on the other hand, had a headache and, truth be told, a slight fear of heights she'd never had occasion to mention to anyone else. Sledding involved hills, some of them steep, so she was in no hurry to get started.

As if dragging her here hadn't been enough, Avery had invited her father's golf buddy to join them. Piper had run into Grayson at the bar, which wasn't really much of a coincidence since anyone in Pine Harbor for more than a day wandered into the Harbor House Bar at some point. Grayson had spotted her right away, seated in a large corner booth in the midst of her half-dozen friends. He'd left the two guys he was chatting with to come over to greet her. By the time Piper had gone around the table to introduce everyone, Avery had managed to invite him to go snow tubing the next day. *Thank you, Avery*.

Even before Grayson became part of the picture, Piper had tried to back out of the whole expedition. She was a little embarrassed by her issue with heights —especially rapid descents from them—so she neglected to mention it. Avery had insisted that the outing would be an essential component to Piper's repatriation to hometown life. So now, with their gear unpacked, Piper turned her full attention to bemoaning her fate, leaving no opportunity to notice Grayson's imported car pulling into the parking lot beside them.

"Well, look who's here." Avery's eyes brightened as Grayson emerged from his car. "Mmm. That shiny black car sets off his blond hair and blue eyes."

Piper tried not to look, but she stole a quick glance. "Have at him."

"You don't want him?" Avery looked truly horrified.

Piper leveled a look. "We're not dividing up Halloween candy here. He's a guy who plays golf with my father. What about that says potential relationship to you?"

"Everything. Good-looking, well-connected. And look at that car. He's got money." Avery eyed Grayson as he unfolded himself from his car. "So if what you're saying is that he's all mine, then okay."

Piper sighed. "He's not mine to give. Are you even listening to me?"

Avery was already moving toward Grayson. "Grayson! Good morning!" Avery reached out her hand and shook his.

He turned to Piper with a smile just as Juan

pulled up and got out of his pickup. With a passing glance toward Piper, Juan's attention was soon drawn into a conversation with the other dozen friends who'd arrived—including Tiffany Tucker, Piper couldn't help but notice. Well, wasn't this little outing turning into quite an event?

Tiffany took the lead. "Shall we?" Without waiting, she hooked her arm into Juan's and trudged up the worn path to the top of the hill. Tiffany's prattle kept him far too occupied to notice Piper a dozen steps behind. That she'd caught herself watching him and wondering what he was saying to Tiffany was not a good sign. She had to stop thinking—obsessing —about him. *It's over. It's been over for years, so stop torturing yourself.*

Piper tore her gaze from Juan only to find Avery cheerfully chattering away with Grayson Endicott. In fact, everyone seemed to be walking in pairs. "All we need is an ark," Piper muttered.

They arrived at the top of the hill, and Piper looked down. Yup. It hadn't changed. She had hoped that she had, but that was one more hope dashed to the rocks. Even if she'd forgotten, the climb up to the top should have reminded her of its height and her childhood fears. But that was the power of romantic obsession, or whatever it was that made her watch

Juan and Tiffany talk their way up to the top of the hill.

Tiffany dragged Juan onto a toboggan behind her. Piper mumbled, "If she scoots back any farther, they'll need a condom."

Avery tucked her hair into her cap. "I'm sorry, what?"

"Nothing." Piper stared at the foot of the hill.

Tiffany and Juan were the first to take off down the slope. Then a few others joined in. Piper gripped the snow-tube handle and urged Avery and Grayson to take the toboggan and go on without her. She waved them off confidently. "I'll be right behind you." *Standing here, planning my exit strategy.* She made a show of sitting on the tube and cheerfully waved, but Grayson came over to her.

"Need a push?"

"No! I've got it." She heard the panic in her own voice and tried to sound calm. "Oh, look. Avery's ready."

He looked over then looked back at Piper. "It's no problem. Ready? One, two..."

"No, really. That's okay." She lifted her palms in protest, but he had already said "three," and her tube was off down the mountain.

While she'd been sledding a few times as a child,

she had never gone down such a steep hill, nor had she ever used a tube. It soon became clear that steering was not really an option. She could only hope the indented path she was on would keep her within its bounds for the rest of her journey downhill.

Grayson and Avery laughed somewhere behind her, while Piper resisted the urge to close her eyes as she prayed for an end to this torment. It eventually came. She could see people at the bottom of the hill picking up their sleds and toboggans and heading back up.

Her tube spun out of control and headed toward a tree off to the side. Heart pounding, she tried to tip over like she would have in a sled, but the tube would not tip. She was more or less wedged in its donut-shaped hole. Between the increasing speed and the sights spinning around her, everything was a blur. She hung on, bracing for impact.

Then it stopped. At first, all she could manage was to breathe for a moment. Then, she opened her eyes and looked up to find Juan staring down at her. She didn't know what was worse—her heart pounding with fear or the shortness of breath. Or maybe it was Juan's concerned look.

He bent down and peered into her eyes. "Are you okay?"

"I'm fine. I just..." Her attempt to rise out of the

tube failed. When she faltered, Juan reached under her arms and scooped her up. She was in his arms, and they stood face-to-face. It was only a couple of moments, but they seemed just this side of eternal. She whispered a thank-you, took a step back, and stumbled.

Juan grasped her arm to steady her. "Are you sure you're okay?"

She took a breath, but before she could answer, Grayson and Avery called out as they headed her way.

Juan glanced at them and looked back at her. "Piper?"

She nodded.

Laughter cut through the air as Avery and Grayson joined them. "C'mon, Pipes! Let's go do it again!"

Grayson's lips parted, but Avery tugged his arm before he could speak, and they were on their way back up the hill.

Piper said, "Excuse me," and left Juan to catch up with the pair. "Avery, I'm sorry, but I've got a migraine coming on. I've got to get home. Do you think you can get a ride home?"

"She's got one now," Grayson replied.

Avery caught Piper's eye. She wasn't buying the migraine excuse, but she had the good sense not to mention it. "Thanks, Grayson. Feel better, Pipes." Avery and Grayson turned and headed back up the hill.

Juan was waiting for Piper, tube in hand, and walked her back to her car. He loaded the tube in the car, closed the hatch, and turned to her, still looking worried. "Are you going to be okay alone?"

Piper nodded and forced a smile. "It's just a migraine. It'll pass."

He looked puzzled. "I don't remember you getting migraines."

She looked into his eyes. She'd never been a good liar, especially not to Juan. "I only get them when I go snow tubing." She didn't even try to hide a sly grin.

"That's a very unique sort of migraine."

"Well, I'm a very unique sort of person." She smiled, but he didn't smile back.

"What's wrong?" He'd always been able to read her, which wasn't a good thing at the moment.

"I don't like heights. And I've just discovered I don't like tubes, either. So rather than spoil anyone else's fun, I'm just going to go home and spend the rest of my afternoon without terror."

For the first time since she'd seen him again, she saw the old warmth and kindness in his eyes. "If you need anything, let me know."

Piper smiled. "Thanks, but I can't imagine what I might need." As she lost herself in his gaze, she suddenly could imagine what she might need.

Juan's eyes softened. "I don't know. I thought maybe a drink might help. You look a bit rattled."

Piper wanted to tell him she was, and it would. But she wasn't sure she could talk and melt at the same time.

An unmistakable voice cried out Juan's name. They turned to find Tiffany making impressive progress toward them through the knee-deep snow. That girl was fit.

Piper indulged in one last look at Juan. "I'll be okay. Thanks."

He shook his head as though it were nothing. Neither seemed able to look away.

That must have been why Tiffany arrived, to provide needed assistance. "There you are, Juan!" As if she'd let him out of her sight for one moment.

Piper said, "See you later."

As Tiffany hooked her arm into Juan's and led him away, she made no effort to lower her voice as she said, "See you *later*?"

Juan said, "Tiff, it's just an expression."

Piper rolled her eyes and went to her car.

FOUR

Piper lay dozing in front of the TV when car lights shone in through the curtains. A car door slammed shut and woke her. She sat up abruptly and looked around before coming fully awake. Not in the mood for company, she got up and peeked through a crack in the curtains, expecting to see Avery and Grayson. It was already dark outside, but the porch light across the driveway came on. Juan was home. She touched her mouth and chin to make sure she hadn't been drooling while sleeping. Juan went inside. From here, it looked like he was alone. It also looked like she was peering through her window to see whether he was alone, which began to feel a little pathetic.

For some reason, Piper had thought moving back home would be some sort of cure. People grew up and changed. She had every reason to believe it would bring things into better focus where Juan was concerned. Unfortunately, while her focus had improved, so had Juan—in every imaginable way, which was the crux of her problem. She couldn't stop remembering how good they once were, and she couldn't help but wonder how good they'd be now. Whenever she got to this point, she would stop and give herself a stern talking to.

This had gone on for years. Anytime a relationship seemed to show any hope, something would happen to remind her of Juan. The first time was with the guy she called the gas man—and not because he was a meter reader by trade. It had all started out so nicely. Set up by a friend, they had met for a coffee. It progressed to a date, and a few more dates followed, until one day, they wound up comfortably situated on the sofa in front of the TV. Pizza and beer and a cozy night in seemed like such a good idea. Then the belching began—because he'd grown so fully at ease in her company, clearly far more than she was with him. The fact that he was oblivious to it made everything worse. Halfway through the film, he moved in for a belch-breath-infused kiss, but Piper had come to a crossroads. She would continue through life without him.

On that night, she suffered her first pretend

migraine. So began her journey down the path of occasional serial lying. With one palm to her forehead and a few well-placed winces, she had the gas man's arms loaded with the box of leftover pizza and the last half of a six-pack of beer. He managed one final and resonant burp before the door closed between them. She never saw—or heard—him again.

There were a few more dating attempts after that. The bobble head was a very good listener, but he gave her motion sickness.

The 'stache stroker was, she supposed, keeping the restaurant floors of America clean by collecting meal particles in his facial foliage, but when she found herself guessing what each fleck of food was, she was done. She went pretty quickly from dodging his kisses to dodging his phone calls.

The wandering eye lasted halfway through the first date. It was like watching tennis as her date's eyes darted from her to assess every boob and behind that walked by—all this while she was talking to him. Piper forfeited the match and left with a migraine.

The fixer-upper was crazy about her. He thought she'd be even more perfect if she straightened her red curls. He once dated this makeup artist who could conceal all those freckles. Did she always wear flats? Could she try heels for their next date? There was no next date.

There were others who, while lacking such memorable traits, all shared one tragic flaw. They weren't Juan.

And so here she was, all alone. That called for some wine. To save herself having to get up for refills, she brought the bottle with her to the sofa and resumed her TV binge watching.

Three episodes later, she got up to go to the bathroom. Only then, standing up, did she realize how much she'd had to drink. She hadn't felt like this since college—and not in a good way. She walked with the overly deliberate care of one who thought she looked sober.

"Dang it. That door's in the way." She sidestepped the door she'd bumped into and returned to season three of her TV series.

PIPER HAD BEEN on Juan's mind all day. He kept seeing the look on her face at the foot of the hill, and he worried. He knew her. Although it had been years, he still knew every expression, every lift of the eyebrow. Something was wrong, and he couldn't let it go. So he finally gave up and went to check on her.

He knocked at the door and waited. And thought. Back there at the foot of the hill, he'd thought way too much about putting his lips against hers. How could he still want her? After years of building what she'd nearly destroyed, he had a life he was proud of, and he had self-respect. He'd always known he was at a disadvantage in some people's eyes. But with Piper, he'd thought it was different. But how could it have been? Back then, there wasn't a Mexican for miles around. He couldn't walk into a store or café without feeling different. Sometimes, he was made to feel that way. Other times, it was only in his mind—and probably theirs. He became good at second-guessing, which often left him assuming the worst. Life was less disappointing that way.

It had taken a while to accept that Piper liked him. They had lived in one another's periphery for years. But then one day, they talked, and things changed after that. He changed. He refused to believe it at first. He was not falling in love. So he kept his distance from her—or he tried. But before long, he was sitting beside her at lunch or the library, and he couldn't help but talk to her then. She was right there and so easy to talk to. Eventually, they just knew where the other would be throughout the day, and they fell into a pattern, like good friends, but not. It was more—a sort of understanding that they were going to be different. And they were. By the time he decided to kiss her, it was long overdue. And electric. Or explosive. Or love.

He'd set himself up for a fall, and that fall was hard. Oh, her father had been so polite to him after the breakup. And why wouldn't he be? He'd gotten his way. Piper would not be brought down in life, burdened with the financial woes of a Mexican manual-laborer husband.

Hadley Harriman had even referred work to Juan after his father had died. He'd helped build Juan's business, perhaps out of guilt. That was just one more thing Juan learned to live with—being grateful and polite to the man who had taken his true love away. He struggled over the years, but he'd finally come to terms with his life and found peace. He wasn't ecstatically happy, but he was content.

So why was he standing here at her door?

Piper opened the door and greeted him a bit too exuberantly.

He furrowed his brow and said, "Are you okay?"

She balked. "Why do you keep asking me that?"

He paused and then quietly said, "I asked you that hours ago, just after you narrowly escaped running into a tree."

"Yeah, and...?"

"I don't know. I just worry about you." He looked into her eyes until he thought he might kiss her, then he looked away and caught sight of an empty wine bottle next to the sofa.

Her long red mop of hair was falling out of its knot, and short wild wisps of curls sprang free from her hairline. She was an adorable mess as she looked up at him with her green eyes wide open. "I think about you too."

Her words set fire to conflicting emotions that caught in his throat. Stopping by here had been a mistake. A huge one. If he didn't leave now... well, he had to leave now. "It looks like you're doing okay. So I'll go."

"Why?" She put her hand on his upper arm and then made a tactile study of his biceps.

Empty wine bottle on the table, an overexuberant greeting, and this. She was drunk. There was no other reason she'd practically throw herself at him. Maybe that wasn't quite what she was doing, but she'd let her guard down. She was vulnerable, standing there, looking at him with her lips parted, so soft and appealing. And he liked it—too much to take advantage of her.

"Busy day tomorrow."

Her eyes filled with disappointment. "Oh, okay. Well, goodbye." She reached up and kissed him on the cheek. Then her arms reached around his neck.

Juan swallowed, gently reached back, and disentangled himself from her arms. He stepped back and held onto her shoulders. "Good night, Piper."

SEVERAL BIRTHDAY PRESENTS were stacked on their table in the Harbor House Bar, where Avery sat surrounded by friends. Grayson sat on one side, and Piper sat next to him. Tiffany arrived a few minutes late. That girl knew how to make an entrance. She dragged over a chair, and before she was done, she'd dislodged three people from their spots so she could wedge her chair in next to Juan's. If Juan had any objection to the whole operation, he hid it.

He also hid any feelings about what had happened last night. Piper may have been tipsy, but she remembered it all. It wasn't like she'd been brazen. It was only a kiss on the cheek and a hug between friends. Her own feelings had blown it out of proportion, but it was a nonevent that meant nothing to Juan. Piper had to move on.

With no warning, Grayson reached under the table, placed his hand on Piper's knee, and gave it a squeeze.

Piper let out a yelp as she swatted his hand away. The table conversation stopped abruptly as everyone stared, including Avery. Rather than ruin her friend's birthday, Piper looked from one puzzled face to the next. "Leg cramp." She proceeded to make a show of rubbing her leg for a moment. "It's okay." The conversation picked up where it left off.

Grayson leaned over and whispered into Piper's ear. "We need to talk."

Piper's smile faded as she turned and gave him a veiled but livid look. "No, Grayson. We don't."

"Call me Gray."

Piper whispered through clenched teeth. "I'll call you a lot more than that if you try that again."

Avery turned and gave Piper a smile. Somehow Piper managed to smile back, but as she did, Grayson managed to move into her field of vision. He smiled as though she'd smiled at him.

As soon as Avery's attention was drawn elsewhere, Grayson turned, but before he could speak, Piper whispered, "It's my friend's birthday party. What's the matter with you?"

He turned back to Avery as if nothing were wrong. But for poor Avery, everything was. Earlier in the day, she'd confided to Piper that she was falling for Grayson. At the time, Piper dismissed it because Avery had always fallen too hard and too fast. After only a few days with Grayson, she was already wearing her heart on her sleeve, if not also on her cuff, her lapel, and her back blue-jeans pocket. Given Grayson's behavior, she was headed for a fall, and Piper refused to contribute to it.

Avery opened the gift card they'd all bought her. "I wasn't expecting this."

Piper looked past Grayson to Avery. *Neither was I.*

Avery thanked everyone profusely and excused herself for a trip to the restroom. Seizing a moment when the others around them were distracted, Grayson whispered, "I need to see you alone, just to talk."

Piper shook her head. "You've said more than enough." She had to hand it to him. He could smolder. He must have practiced in front of a mirror.

"God, you're driving me crazy."

Piper couldn't hold his gaze. "So are you. But not in a good way."

Grayson had the nerve to laugh. Avery slid along the bench to her place beside Grayson. "What's so funny?"

Avery shrugged. "I'll let him tell you." She turned away to the two people between her and the end of the booth. "Would you please excuse me?" She headed straight for the restroom. A few minutes later, she emerged with renewed composure and managed to position herself at the end of the booth, two people over from Grayson. Of course, this put her right next to Tiffany, but there was no such thing as perfect.

After a few rounds of drinks, Tiffany got up and said her goodbyes. Someone asked Juan if she was okay, which drew a confused look and a shrug from Juan. "Yeah, she's got to go teach a Piloxing class."

Avery said, "A what?"

"She says it's like a combination of Pilates and boxing. I don't know. I just know she teaches it five times a week."

Avery nodded. "Oh, okay. I thought something was wrong when she left so abruptly."

Juan squinted. "Wrong?"

"You know, between you two."

Juan shook his head. "Us two?" He narrowed his eyes and regarded Avery as though she'd lost her mind.

Avery shrugged it off. "Oh. Well, whatever."

As the party broke up, Avery looked out the window. "It's snowing!" She turned and announced, "First snow in January. You know what that means. Snolleyball tomorrow!"

Grayson wrinkled his eyebrows. "What?"

"Snow volleyball. It's an annual tradition. You'll have to come play."

"I will?"

She took hold of his arm and drew closer. "Yes, you will."

Piper listened to the exchange and tried not to grimace as she fastened the front of her coat. She looked up to find Juan before her, pulling on his gloves. "Did you drive here?"

"No, I walked." It made sense since they only lived a few streets away.

Grayson seemed to appear out of nowhere. "I'll give you a ride."

"No, thanks." Piper couldn't get that out fast enough.

The sharp edge to her tone seemed to catch Juan's attention. He studied her for a moment and turned to Grayson. "We're walking together."

Grayson opened his mouth as if he might say something, but Piper was quicker. "Yeah, ready?" She looked at Juan and made a dash for the door. If they walked briskly enough, they might turn the corner to their street before Grayson got to his car and pulled out of the parking lot.

Once outside, Piper tucked her scarf inside her collar. "It's cold out."

Juan looked at her sideways. "It's winter."

Piper smirked. "Yes, but... never mind." They walked in silence for a while. "I hope Avery had a happy birthday."

"I'm sure she did." Juan stopped walking. "But you didn't. Piper, what's wrong?"

She shrugged unconvincingly. "Wrong? Nothing."

He studied her. "There just seemed to be something with Grayson. Has he done something to upset you?"

"No."

"Oh. Must be your leg cramp." He studied her but didn't press the issue.

A car pulled out of the parking lot a half block behind them. Piper picked up her pace. "C'mon. It's cold out. Let's go home."

Juan peered at her for a moment, then resumed walking. After a few more minutes of silence, they arrived at the driveway and stood between their two homes.

"Well, thanks for walking me home." She turned toward the lodge.

"Wait. Piper, look... if he's bothering you..."

She shook her head. "It's nothing."

Juan looked away, shaking his head. "How well do you know him?"

She shrugged. "He plays golf with my father."

"I think you should avoid him."

"Do you?" Despite the fact that he echoed her own thoughts, hearing this coming from Juan, who had made it clear only last night how he felt—or didn't feel—put her on the defensive to an extent that surprised even Piper. "Well, thank you, but that's not your call."

"I know. I just don't like the way he looks at you. And I don't like the way you look when he's looking at you—or talking to you." Juan turned his troubled expression away.

It took Piper a moment to be able to speak. "When did you even have time to notice how he looked at me, with Tiffany commanding so much of your attention?"

He looked nonplussed. "Tiffany? What does she have to do with this?"

"Nothing."

Juan combed his fingers through his hair. "We were talking about Grayson."

"And now we're not." She turned and tossed a "good night" over her shoulder. She wasn't sure who she was more agitated by, Grayson or Juan—or maybe herself. But Juan was here, so he got the brunt of it. Even as she was walking away, she knew that she'd overreacted, but she couldn't seem to help it. She fidgeted with the key and finally unlocked the door. When she turned to close it, Juan was still standing there in that casual way of his that had always calmed her. With a hint of annoyance lingering in her tone, she said, "Okay, I'm sorry."

It was too dark to see, but if she knew Juan, he was starting to smile. "For what?" As if he didn't know.

"What I said. Everything."

His stance relaxed just a bit.

"Except Tiffany. She hasn't changed much." Piper knew she was better than that, but it just came out.

Juan walked the few steps it took to stand in front of her. "Don't worry about Tiffany."

Piper bristled. "I'm not worried."

"Or Grayson."

She couldn't quite say she wasn't worried about him. Maybe worried was too strong a word.

Juan said quietly, "I'm not your enemy. I hope we're still friends."

Still friends? That's not quite what we were. "Sure. Of course."

The porch light caught part of his smile and maybe a trace of longing. "Good."

He held her gaze for what felt like an hour-long second. "Well, good night." He left.

"Good night." Piper nodded as if anyone could see. She turned and closed the door behind her. "Friend."

Why did it sound like a death knell? Friend was not the worst thing he could have called her. Or the best. *Don't overthink it.*

Piper fell asleep, counting the seconds that Juan had gazed into her eyes.

FIVE

Fresh snow on a Saturday morning meant only one thing—the big snolleyball game. Piper pulled on her gloves and stayed close to any group that didn't include Grayson. But as they split up into teams, Tiffany demonstrated a startling grasp of math that had gone undetected in high school. "We've got one too many. Piper! Why don't you go play on the other team to even things out?"

"Well, I..." But there was nothing to say that wouldn't make matters worse. She couldn't exactly announce that she was avoiding Grayson or that she'd rather be closer to Juan. Neither man wanted to hear it. And while Grayson was certainly annoying enough, publicly insulting him would not sit well with Avery, who was still under his spell. So Piper took her place on the other side of the net. At least she managed to maneuver herself into a position as far away from Grayson as one could be while still playing on the same team.

But that left her mind free to dwell on thoughts of Juan. It didn't help that he wore a red fleece jacket that caught her eye whenever he moved, or that he looked so good in it. Although, he wasn't moving when Tiffany spiked the ball onto Piper's head. She was stunned for the moment it took Tiffany and Juan to rush over and help her to a nearby folding chair.

Once Piper was comfortably seated, Juan went to get her some water. While he was gone, Tiffany sounded uncharacteristically compassionate as she said, "I'm so sorry! I should have taken it easy on you. That extra five pounds must have slowed down your reflexes."

"My extra what?" Piper scowled. *Actually, it's seven, but thanks for noticing, Tiffany.*

Juan arrived just in time for his presence to deter Piper from lunging—extra five pounds and all—at Tiffany's throat. In her mind. Piper wasn't about to engage in hand-to-hand combat with the likes of Tiffany, mainly because she taught Piloxing classes five days a week and could kick Piper's butt to New Hampshire.

Juan peered into Piper's eyes. "How many fingers am I holding up?"

"Twelve. See? I'm fine." Piper set down the water cup. "Let's get back to the game."

Juan bent down until they were face-to-face. "I'm benching you."

"But—"

Juan shook his head. "Just sit here and watch us make fools of ourselves."

Truth be told, Piper's head did feel a little bit tingly, so she complied, but she didn't enjoy it. Now, there was no way to escape seeing Tiffany in action. Every wide-eyed look, every flirtatious touch was on display—not only for Juan's benefit, but for Piper's. Piper muttered, "Why not just spray your territory and be done with it?"

Grayson plopped down beside her as both teams took a break. "Spray what?"

"Oh, nothing. I was just talking to myself."

"About what?"

Piper turned with a bland look on her face and said dryly, "Shopping list. Spray... uh... cooking oil, a dozen eggs, quart of milk, and... oh, what am I forgetting? Oh, yes." His attention span was even shorter than she'd suspected. Before she'd even gotten to loaf of bread, he was gone in search of a better conversation. And he found it with Tiffany. God only knew—

and Piper didn't really care—what they found to talk about. She was just happy they did.

Juan came over with a bottle of water and crouched by Piper's chair. "How are you feeling?"

"I'm fine."

"Are you sure?"

"Positive." Maybe Tiffany had done Piper a favor. This was the most attention she'd gotten from Juan since she'd come home. Her medical advisor gave her permission to rejoin the game, which was good, because she had no intention of sitting in the cold for the rest of the day.

A half hour later, Piper's team was actually winning. Grayson turned out to have played beach volleyball competitively, so she began to appreciate him—but only in this narrow context. She warmed to him even more when he put Tiffany's volleyball skills to the test, until she realized that a bit more than the spirit of athletic competition blazed in their eyes. Juan didn't seem to care that Tiffany's interest had strayed, but Piper caught Avery watching while Grayson and Tiffany shared a look. If Piper could pick up on the chemistry, Avery certainly could. This day would not end well for her friend.

On the plus side, Grayson had moved on and left dreams of Piper behind, which would spare her from being the third angle of a love triangle, which, however obtuse, could have cost her a friend.

IF THERE WAS any greater tradition than the annual snolleyball match, it was the after-game drink at the Harbor House Bar. Tiffany and Grayson made no secret of their newfound affection, which left Piper handing tissues to Avery. As her friend surreptitiously blotted her tears, she said, "I can't do this, just sit here and watch them canoodle all evening." She started to get up, but Piper pulled her down by the elbow.

"Just take a breath. Don't do anything you'll regret."

Avery leaned back and looked at Piper as though she had just lost her mind. "I wasn't gonna go get an axe from my trunk."

"Good."

"It's in my purse."

They both laughed, but Avery's laughter soon came with tears. "I just want to go home. Look, I'm going to pretend to go to the restroom, but I'm actually going to escape through the back exit, so let's say goodbye now."

Piper started to get up. "I'll go with you."

"Aw, Pipes. You're the best. But I just need to go home and have a big ugly cry. By myself." She smiled through teary eyes. "But thank you for being willing to endure the flash flood of mucus and tears that will be me in about fifteen minutes."

Piper gave her a sympathetic look, squeezed her hand, and said, "I understand."

With that, Avery turned and left undetected except, evidently, by Juan, who appeared at Piper's table and set down two beers before slipping into Avery's vacated seat. The two of them sat side by side on the bench by the wall and watched everyone else.

Juan took a drink and leaned back. "She'll get over it."

At the sight of Tiffany throwing her fit little arms about Grayson, Piper smirked and turned to face Juan. "So will you."

"Me?"

Piper wrinkled her face. "Uh, yeah."

"Uh, no." He leaned toward her, peering intently. "Did you think she and I were...?"

"Yeah, because... weren't you?"

"No!" He looked away, rolling his eyes, and then looked back at Piper.

The glint in his eyes troubled Piper but not

nearly as much as what he said next. His mouth started to spread into a smile. "Were you jealous?"

It didn't help her case any that she stared slack-jawed while she failed to form any defense. The best she could manage was an exaggerated protest and the lamest possible "no."

Suddenly, everything changed. Juan's amusement faded as he searched Piper's eyes.

She felt breathless but managed somehow to speak. "It's been eight years." She meant it as proof that she could not have been jealous, because... jealousy expired after seven?

That was not how he took it, apparently. For one unguarded moment, they gazed into each other's eyes, and the truth passed between them as surely as if they had said it out loud to each other. There was something there still.

Then Grayson and Tiffany plopped down at their table and killed it. That window of time when they might have broken through the polite anguish they both carried around was now gone. Only silent tension remained.

Grayson gave Piper a look that she couldn't quite read. It had a sort of "you had your chance" vibe that made her want to laugh in his face. But she took the high road and ignored him.

Tiffany said, "You two look very cozy."

Juan leaned back comfortably. "Do we?"

Tiffany smiled. "No hard feelings, then?"

"Why would there be?"

She shrugged. "No reason." She turned to Grayson. "Oh look, people are dancing. Let's go!" And they were gone as quickly as they'd arrived.

Piper watched their departure. "Sometimes things just work out for the best."

"Sometimes." Juan was looking at her with that penetrating gaze that made her heart ache and yet yearn for more.

"What happened to us?" The words just came out of her mouth, and judging by the look on Juan's face, they shouldn't have. He had that look—like he'd just seen a ghost. The ghost of *What-the-Heck-Was-I-Thinking* Past. That was a hard ghost to shake. And she had just summoned its spirit. She hadn't meant to broach the subject. This wasn't the right place or time to have this conversation, so she made a good effort to backtrack. "Sorry. It must've been that volleyball blow to the head."

This would have been a great time for Juan to say something to put her at ease, but he didn't. He just sat there. It was Piper's own fault. She had opened the wound with no warning—just yanked out the sutures—and now every emotion they'd felt on the night of their parting spilled out, perfectly preserved and painfully palpable.

"It's late. Good night, Piper." And he left.

Piper felt sick to her stomach. The music was blaring, and the lights blurred together. She gave Juan enough time to get to his car and drive off, then she slipped away and headed for home.

SIX

Piper set down her purse and sank into the sofa. She scrolled down the phone screen and selected her "Men Suck" playlist. With that done, she dashed off a commiserative text to Avery and picked up a book. Two pages later, she set it back down, having no idea what she'd just read. It was no use.

She leaned her head back on the sofa. Eyes closed, she replayed the worst part of her evening. And yet, there had been moments... like the moment Juan had just walked over from the bar and sat down beside her as if it were perfectly natural. For an instant, it had been. She felt the old sense of belonging she'd once felt in his presence. Before they expressed it in words, there had been a tacit awareness of something between them that she now knew was rare. It wasn't so much a magnetic attraction as it was a knowledge that they were connected somehow. It was there from the start without thought, like the sun and the wind. But like other forces of nature, it held the power to destroy its most perfect creations. And as young as they were, they didn't know enough to worry about it. They hadn't known heartache.

With her head filled with memories and regret, Piper dozed off.

A knock at the door awoke her. She looked through the peephole and opened the door. "Juan?" His eyes were fraught with emotion. Piper stepped aside, and he walked in and looked around before his burning gaze settled on Piper.

Having never seen him like this, Piper assumed the worst. Someone had died. But his parents were already gone, and he had no brothers or sisters. Then it struck her. He was in her parents' house. Something had happened to her parents, and their house phone was the number they had in their wallets.

She didn't want to know, because then it would be real. Her voice was quiet and strained. "What's happened?"

"To us?" He stood, barely moving, and his eyes tightened with bitterness. "Isn't that what you wanted to know? What happened to us?"

It took Piper a moment to shift gears from fear that her parents were hurt to relief that they weren't, and then to the realization of Juan's meaning. This was the conversation she'd both wanted and dreaded. Her lips parted to speak, but he interrupted.

"How could you ask me that?" His voice wasn't loud, but he spoke with such intensity he might as well have been shouting. "You."

Without thinking, Piper took a step back, which drew Juan closer. He gazed into her eyes with unsettling force. "You happened to us."

Piper shook her head as if denying the truth, and its results could absolve her of guilt for the years of pain and resentment she saw in his eyes.

He took another step toward her. Now inches away, he could barely get the words out past the bitterness that choked him. "I. Loved. You."

He was fuming. She knew it, but his lips were so close to hers that she must have moved closer—or maybe he did. Maybe neither could resist the desire to taste what they'd remembered for so many years. Piper gave in to the feel of his lips against hers. Their lips parted, and if a kiss could devour years of heartache and regret, theirs nearly succeeded.

She pressed her body against his and ran her hands along his shoulders and down his chest. Not only didn't he stop her, he circled his strong arms about her and pulled her against him.

Her voice came out in a husky whisper. "I never stopped loving you."

His whole body straightened, and he gently pushed her away to arm's length. Piper didn't know what to think, let alone what to do. She hoped he would say something to explain why he'd come here to make her heart pound like this, only to put distance between them.

He stared at her as if she were toxic. "I didn't come here for this. I don't want it. I don't want us." His eyes darted about before settling on her. "You made your choice."

In his current state, anything she said would only make it worse, so she watched him and listened.

He shook his head. "I thought I'd left it behind. I'm an adult. I thought we could at least try to be friends."

"Well, we're not doing a very good job of it." Her words just came out with no thought. But there was unfinished business between them. The air had been charged since she first saw him again. They couldn't be near one another without feeling it.

Juan's eyes locked onto hers. "It's too late."

"For what?"

"Anything." Juan peered into her eyes as though she'd gone mad. "Us. Friendship. It's all a mistake. There's no use in pretending otherwise."

That stung. Her eyes narrowed as she thought of the kind things he'd done since her return. There had been moments when she'd dared to hope. "Well, you're very good at pretending."

"I wonder where I learned that?"

The blow landed. He seemed determined to break her heart again. And he was succeeding. But this time, it was worse than before.

When she'd gone off to college, she'd spent weeks waiting for him to contact her. Waiting had turned to diminishing hope, and hope died. Her world became small as she went between dorm room and class. While everyone was enjoying their first taste of freedom away from home, she was retreating to give in to despair.

Now her heart was wide open and breaking. She couldn't go through that again. "I think you should go." She expected him to walk out the door, but he stayed.

"I will. When I'm finished." He regained his composure.

Now back on track, apparently acting out the scene he'd rehearsed in his head, he said, "What happened to us? Yeah, I wondered about that myself. We had something that was perfect and true. You said you would marry me." He lowered his voice. "You said that you loved me."

"I did." *I still do.*

"But your father said no. Because God forbid you should marry a Mexican. Or was it because I wasn't a snooty rich bastard like the summer yacht-sailing crowd he so loved to hang out with? My family didn't come over on the Mayflower. My great-grandfather came over the border—legally, by the way—during the Mexican Revolution, when his factory was shut down. He worked in the shipping industry and landed up here in Maine, where he spent the rest of his life building a business. My father took over from him. He was proud of what he and his father had built with their rough, working-man's hands, and he taught me to work hard like them, to love my family, and to do the right thing. He told me one day the business would be mine. It was my heritage and my future—a proud one.

"True, at the time, I had little to offer you but my love and my life, but it would have been yours. I knew there would be more, but you weren't willing to wait. Or maybe you just didn't have faith that I'd take care of you."

"I didn't want to be taken care of." Piper wanted to flee, but he'd forced it all out in the open. There was no turning back. "You would have had me living in your parents' home—one more mouth to feed. And how long would it have been before I got pregnant?

And just when was school going to happen for me? When was I going to have my own life and my own independence?"

"We could have worked it out."

"How? My father would never have allowed it. He would have disowned me. I couldn't just turn from my family." She hesitated. "It would have broken his heart to see me living like that."

Juan folded his arms across his chest and nodded. "And that's what really happened to us. You didn't want to break his heart, so you broke mine instead."

Piper looked him in the eye. "I wanted to go to college. I wanted it."

"I could have put you through college. I've had enough for a couple of years to pay cash for any college you could have wanted. Would waiting five or six years have derailed the grand path to success you're on now?"

She leaned away from the sting of his words. "That's not fair. I've just had a small setback."

Juan nodded. "Yeah? So did I, and that setback was you." He raked his fingers through his hair. "But I survived and moved on. And you went on to become an unemployed accountant living in your parents' basement—oh, sorry, guest cottage. Good for you, Piper. I hope it was worth it."

"Why are you trying to hurt me?"

"Because you had to ask. I was fine. But that wasn't enough. You had to dissect our relationship like some OCD lab tech, to see what was inside. Well, here's your answer—nothing. It took me a while, but I'm over you, Piper."

She nodded. "I get it. Well, that was some 'over you' kiss you gave me."

He glanced away then looked into her eyes. "That was just two people acting on remembered emotions. Those feelings are like ghosts. They're not real."

Juan looked into her eyes long enough for his loathing to settle deep in her heart, then he walked out and closed the door firmly behind him.

BRIGHT MORNING SUNLIGHT streamed in through the window as Piper stirred and got out of bed, squinting. As she pulled on a robe and slid her feet into her slippers, she looked at her matted hair in the mirror and then looked away, rolling her eyes. As a second knock sounded on the door, she tiptoed into the living room, treading lightly to minimize any squeaking of the floorboards.

"Pipes, I know you're in there. Your car's parked out here."

Piper sighed with relief to hear Avery's voice. At least it wasn't Juan. She still felt the stab of his last look of contempt. She couldn't take any more—at least not today—not until last night's wounds had formed scars.

"Pi—"

She opened the door as Avery yelled the last half of her name in her face.

"Sorry." She walked in without being invited—not that Piper would have turned her away—and she held out a pressed cardboard drink tray. "Here. Coffee and donuts. I figured you'd go for the coffee, and I could use something sweet—and lots of it. I hate men. They're all just big bundles of muscles and members, with tiny little brains on top just for looks. They sure don't use them for thinking." She plopped down on a chair and devoured a donut.

When Piper wasn't drinking her coffee, she was staring at it with a furrowed brow and unwavering focus.

With her donut dispatched, Avery looked up at Piper. "Oh my gosh, you look awful."

Piper looked at her friend and wished she'd had two cups of coffee before having to converse. But she hadn't, so, still barely awake, she just narrowed her eyes in confusion and stared at her coffee. "I like to think outward appearance is a reflection of one's mental stability." She lifted her eyes to gaze wryly at Avery.

"Oh." Avery blinked. A few moments later, she emerged from a state of deep thought. "Well, I got your text."

Piper thought back on the previous night. Oh yeah, she might have drunk-texted Avery before going to bed.

"So, I thought, since we were both dumped last night, we could do something today to distract us."

"Like hate men?"

Avery's eyebrows creased. "Well, yeah, that's one option."

Piper took a long drink of coffee. "Good. I like facing the day with a plan."

Avery let out a nervous laugh. "Yeah, well, I meant going out. We could do something that involves—"

"No."

"No?"

"Yes. Because if we go out, there's a good chance I'll see *him*—that person whose name I won't say without adding 'that blanking blank blank.'"

Avery winced. "What is this, *Wheel of Fortune*?"

"No, because my fortune sucks." Piper set down her coffee.

Avery pouted in sympathy. "I know how you

feel. By the way, I was dumped, sort of, last night. Not dumped, exactly, since we were never really together. But I wanted to be, so it felt like a dumping."

Piper was too busy twisting her donut napkin to notice Avery's eyes tearing up. "Grayson's an ass."

She looked up to find Avery smiling through her tears. "Thank you."

"You're welcome?" Piper offered a feeble smile.

"You're so right. He deserves Tiffany. And he's an ass. Have we talked about that?" Avery took in a breath and let out a futile sigh. "I wish I could say the same about Juan, but, I'm sorry, he's not."

Piper shook her head. "That's okay. The truth is, I don't really think Juan's a blanking blank blank. Are you ready to solve the puzzle?"

Avery grinned. "Pretty sure I've figured it out."

Piper gazed out the window at the sea, then turned back. "Juan's a man—a real man."

With a knowing nod, Avery said, "A real manly man. Are we playing word games again? Because I could go on. But first—do you have a knife?"

"Avery, don't you think that's a little extreme?"

"Not to hurt anyone! A butter knife."

Piper went to the kitchen and brought back a knife. Avery took it and proceeded to cut a bite-sized piece out of one of the donuts. Then she left it and ate the rest of the donut.

When she glanced over, mouth full of donut, she saw Piper's questioning look. "Well, I didn't want to eat the last one."

"Thanks."

"You're welcome." Avery brushed donut crumbs from her chest. "So, where were we? Ah, yes. Let's go out. The fresh air will do you good."

Piper glanced at the window. "You know... people say that, but I don't see how cold air can cure a broken heart."

Avery shrugged. "It's a distraction."

Piper's eyes opened wide as she suddenly pointed to the window. "Look over there!"

Avery sat up tall and peered toward the window. "What?"

"That was a distraction. Do you feel any better? Is Grayson any less of an ass?"

She was answered with a frown. "Well, maybe it doesn't work unless you get farther away."

"In that case, I'd better make sure my passport's up to date." Piper got up and cleared the empty coffee cups and donut box from the table. "Look, I appreciate what you're trying to do, but it's going to take more than a walk in the park for me to get over Juan."

"I know, Pipes, but it's better than what you had planned."

Piper balked. "You don't know what I had planned."

"Oh, I think I do. Let's see... you're far too despondent to get up and change discs, so my guess is you were planning to beach yourself on the sofa with your bed pillow and blanket and watch whatever was streaming—probably something dystopian taking place in a world of dull earth tones that feels just like your heart."

"Joyless and powerless?" Piper shrugged in agreement. "Only the chosen ones will survive—not the story, but the cruel hourly test that restricts one's needs to a mere twenty-second interval. Sometimes there can be only one."

"Highlander?"

"Snack or bathroom." Piper reached for the remote, but Avery hooked elbows and spun her around. "Not so fast."

Piper rolled her eyes and heaved a sigh. "What, are we square dancing now?"

"Come on, Pipes. Go get dressed. This will be so much fun."

"What will?"

"Oh, I can't tell you that."

"Why, because you have to think of it first?" Piper lifted her eyebrows and smiled.

Avery's shoulders dropped in defeat. "Yeah." Her phone chimed. For a moment, she stared at the screen. "Hey, that nor'easter that was supposed to stay offshore just turned and is heading our way."

"What?"

"Yeah, so I guess our fun activity is going to the store to stock up on essentials for tomorrow."

"Wine, chocolate, and batteries?"

"Yeah, something like that. So get out of that bathrobe. We're going out!"

SEVEN

Soup simmered in the slow cooker as Piper brought in the last armload of firewood. A fire crackled in the fireplace as she poured herself a steaming cup of coffee and breathed in its scent as it mingled with wood smoke. She settled into her favorite chair nestled in the corner by a window. Outside, large flakes of snow drifted down to the ground and to the ocean beyond it as she finished arranging a soft throw blanket over her lap and picked up a book. This was a not-so-bad moment in the midst of a not-so-good winter.

JUAN'S STORM preparedness entailed bringing a case of beer up from the basement and loading it into the fridge. That, a dozen frozen pizzas, and a generous stock of chips and queso would carry him through the storm. He went upstairs to turn up the heat. If the power went out from the storm, he wanted to have a warm house to begin with.

A sight caught his eyes as he walked past a second-floor window. Piper was curled up on the window seat, reading. She looked warm and untroubled, and he wished he was there. A pang of guilt seized him. However justified he might have been to feel as he did toward her, she'd had every right to make the choices she'd made. Unloading on her eight years later did no one any good.

He couldn't entirely blame her—or even her father. At the time, Juan showed no promise of being able to support Piper, which he would have had to do, at least to some degree, if she did not go to college. In this small coastal town, any jobs that existed for unskilled workers would not have paid well. Piper knew that too, and she'd always known she was going to college. Who was he to expect her to give up her dreams so he could pursue his?

Juan's aspirations had been simple—work hard and love Piper. That would have been enough. But when Piper left him, his confidence shifted, or maybe it was only his pride. Either way, after that, he was compelled to succeed. Maybe it was so he could show her and her father how wrong they had been about him. Soon after his twentieth birthday, he lost his mother to cancer. Unable to bear the weight of his grief, his father followed soon after. Juan was alone. He took the small nest egg his father had set aside and, combined with the life insurance, went to college at night. He invested the rest.

As he worked hard to bury his loneliness, his earnings and investments kept growing. And now, here he was. He had weathered losing his girlfriend and both of his parents. Years later, the deepest ache had subsided, allowing him to get through his days feeling practically normal. He had more than enough work to keep him busy and more than enough money to feel comfortable. But he still felt adrift.

He couldn't decide whether it helped or hurt more to see Piper over there now, across the great divide of their shared driveway. The connection between them had somehow survived through the years as though nothing had changed. Who he was had not changed, either. He might have bootstrapped himself to success and social standing within their small town, but he was still the same Juan in Hadley's eyes. Since the breakup, he'd been warm and amiable toward Juan, no doubt because Piper had chosen to leave him behind. He was no longer a threat—as long as he kept a safe distance from his daughter. If Piper had stayed with him years ago, Juan would have had to live with Hadley's constant disapproval. Piper was too influenced by him, and that would have meant constant friction. So maybe it was all for the best.

It was all for the best—if Juan had lost his mind. He walked away from the window. Despite the old pain and resentment, he loved her. It was like trying to deny the sun. He may have locked his heart away from it, but when she came back to town, she came back into his life. Through the years in between, the sun had not stopped shining. And now that he saw Piper each day, the same feelings were there whether he chose to admit or deny them.

He paused at a window downstairs and looked across to the lodge. He was seized with desire to set things right and apologize. He'd berated her and then left the rancor between them to fester. Guilt had nagged him ever since. All the feelings he thought he'd resolved over the years had come up to the surface. When he held Piper's face in his hands, he was back in high school wanting the girl he couldn't have. Back then, he had an excuse, but he knew better now. He was not fortune's fool. He'd done this to himself. And he'd treated her badly. He needed to make it right.

Or maybe he just needed to see her. He moved

toward the door then stopped. Was it too soon—or not soon enough? What if she refused to talk to him? He headed for the kitchen. Dusk was settling in, and he hadn't had lunch yet. That would get his mind off her. He stopped. No, it had to be done. He went to the door and pulled his jacket off the hook.

A small black sports car fishtailed its way into the driveway and parked at the lodge. Juan watched Grayson get out and tromp through foot-deep snow to Piper's door. She answered it wearing a knee-length oversized sweatshirt. Her hair was pulled up into a haphazard knot on her head with red curls escaping in every direction. She looked adorable and in no way expecting Grayson or anyone else. Juan felt a wave of nausea as Piper invited Grayson in and closed the door.

For the next thirty minutes, Juan sat at the counter, beer in hand, ignoring the basketball game on the small mounted TV. If Grayson didn't get his ass in gear and head out, he'd be stuck overnight. Unless Juan cleared the driveway.

Twenty minutes later, Juan closed the garage door on the snow blower and went to the lodge. He'd cut a clean path to the road that even Grayson's sports car couldn't fail to get through. He'd do it again if he had to. And he might, for the snow had picked up.

Just in case she was too busy to notice the newly cleared driveway, Juan went to Piper's door and knocked.

"Juan!" She looked happy to see him, although she was like that—polite.

"Hi, Piper."

"Come in." She looked as though something were on her mind. Or she'd invited him in to save heat. There was no point in reading too much into it. He stepped inside and nodded at Grayson, in full man-spread mode on the sofa as if he were lord of the manor with a beer for a scepter.

Juan looked back at Piper, who was staring expectantly. "Oh, I just wanted to let you know that the driveway's clear now." *In case you couldn't hear the snow thrower mere feet from your door.*

"Oh, thanks." She looked into his eyes as she widened hers.

Knowing her, he was supposed to glean something from that. He just couldn't tell what. Juan narrowed his eyes and looked back more intently. It was like the ultimate game of charades, without actions.

Juan said, "Uh, yeah... it's snowing harder. So there's a limited window of time to get out." He glanced toward Grayson, who was transfixed by the same game Juan had tried to watch earlier. Grayson

let out a cheer that drowned out the conversation at
the door.

Piper leaned close and said softly, "He won't
leave."

Glad to be finished with eyelid charades, Juan
caught on and spoke loudly. "So, Grayson, I was just
telling Piper you've got about a fifteen-minute
window before the snow's too deep to drive through."

Without waiting for a response, Piper got
Grayson's jacket and held it out. "Thanks for
checking up on me, Grayson. Drive safely."

Grayson was a lot of things, but stupid was not
one of them. Annoyed as he was, at the moment, he
didn't put up much of a fight. Plans thwarted, he
accepted defeat, said goodbye to Juan, and kissed
Piper on the cheek. She hid her displeasure as
Grayson walked outside, followed by Piper and Juan.
They sent Grayson off with a wave.

JUAN STOOD OUTSIDE WITH PIPER, who
was clad in her sweatshirt, leggings, and slippers and
hugging herself for warmth. He would have been
happy to take over the task.

Grayson pulled out of the driveway.

"Thank you. I'm sorry you had to do that.

Considering... everything, I had no right to ask."

Juan shook his head. "You didn't ask, exactly."

Piper wrinkled her face. "Well, I did really loudly with thinking."

"Yeah, I guess I kind of heard you." Juan couldn't help but smile. He still remembered each lift of an eyebrow, every facial expression. "Look, about the other day..."

"That's okay." Her eyes flitted downward.

"No, it's not okay." He leveled a frank look.

Piper lifted her eyes to meet his with that combination of softness and strength that he'd always been drawn to. "You had every right to feel that way." She looked guilty and vulnerable—everything he'd once wished to force out of her. Now it only made him feel like less of a person for having unloaded on her.

She shivered. Juan's knee-jerk response was to reach out and pull her against him for warmth, but he caught himself. "Look, you're freezing out here. Go inside. We can talk some other time."

She glanced toward the door and back at him. She hesitated, then said, "How 'bout now?"

Because he wasn't expecting it, he didn't speak for a moment. "Okay."

She smiled softly. "Good. Some hot chocolate will warm us up. Or would you rather have something stronger?"

"Stronger." He grinned and then turned to put his jacket on the hook where Grayson's had been. Piper was already pouring their drinks when he arrived at the counter and sat on a stool.

"Looks like Grayson had the last beer." Piper closed the fridge door. "So... I've got Scotch or, uh, Scotch."

"Scotch is good."

She gave him his drink and waved him on toward the sofa that faced the fireplace flanked by windows on each side that looked out toward the sea. But the only view was of snow being tossed under the outdoor floodlights.

Piper made her way to the sofa and sat beside Juan. "We could have used some of this snow before Christmas. By January, I'm over it."

"Piper, I'm sorry." He could see he'd made her nervous. She was making too much of a point of watching the snow through the window. He'd been impatient. But he'd already begun, so he pressed on. "I didn't like the way I left things last night. Maybe I was saying what I'd wanted to say years ago. But that's no excuse."

"It was because you're Mexican. And because you didn't come from money." Piper stared into the fire.

Juan barely moved, and yet something veiled his

gaze, something dormant that she'd brought back to life. All the words people say, all the names and the looks are tucked away somewhere with the pain that they cause. But this one ached all the more for having come from someone he loved.

Piper took her time before speaking. "I didn't care who you were or where you were from. I loved you."

"I know. Just not enough to stand up to your father."

"You make it sound easy, but I was young, and I wasn't strong and sure of myself like you were. And I knew that my father was just doing what he thought was best."

"Yeah. Because he didn't have to live with his decision."

Juan took a drink and leaned back to stare at the fire. He couldn't look at Piper right now. If he did, she would see everything that he felt—all the anger and resentment... and love. And he would have to face the look of guilt on her face. More than anything else, that look was like a blunt blow to the heart, leaving him with an ache he could barely endure.

"Juan."

He forced himself to look at her, knowing he was too hurt to be guarded.

Piper set down her glass. "I would have been

better off if I'd defied my father. I see now that it could have worked out. But at the time, how could I know? I did want college, and I wanted a career. I didn't know I would fail at it."

"You haven't failed. You were laid off."

"I know. But I guess I'm just trying to say that you were right. I was wrong. And I wish you'd forgive me."

It didn't feel to Juan like the victory he'd expected. While she hadn't come crawling back on her knees like he'd once wished for, time had helped him to let go of the pain. "I do. I forgive you."

Piper looked into his eyes, and he saw the same pain he'd been feeling. "I was such a dreamer. I guess that's another word for fool. I thought I could go to school and you'd be here waiting for me until I was done. I thought I could have it all."

"You could have. But I was hurt, and I was proud." He shook his head.

Piper turned to face Juan. "Losing my job didn't hurt half as much as having you hate me."

"It's never been hate."

Piper heaved a sigh. "Well, it looks like you could use a refill." She reached for the glass, but he reached out to stop her. She looked at his hand, still on her wrist, and her eyes trailed up to his.

Regret overtook him. "I lied to you, Piper." She

looked worried, so he hastened to add, "I never got over you."

"Juan. You can't say things like that unless—"

"Unless I mean it?"

She looked as if she were in shock. She slipped her wrist from his grasp and went to the window, where she folded her arms and wiped her eyes. She stared out at the snow. He remembered how much she hated being out of control, so he leaned back and gave her the time that she needed. He'd waited eight years for her. Now that they were so close, he could wait for her to be ready.

Without turning, she said, "I've always loved you. But I'd given up hope."

He got up and went to her. "It's okay to hope now."

"Really?" She turned around, still looking reluctant.

He held out his arms, and she flew into them. Her lips touched his, and his heart opened up. He pressed his lips to hers and kissed her, held her head in his palm and kissed her again. He had dreamed of a moment like this, but hadn't dared hope it could happen.

He held her in his arms, and his lips brushed her ear. "Would it be awful if I were snowed in and couldn't go home till tomorrow?"

She smiled softly. "Unless you've tied a rope to your door to guide you back home through this blizzard, I'm afraid you're stuck here for the night."

There was nothing to say after that. He kissed her, scooped her up into his arms, and carried her into the bedroom.

PIPER AWOKE in Juan's arms. She took in a breath and sank into his warmth and that scent that belonged only to him. His strong body fitted so perfectly to hers. She reveled in the smooth touch of skin against skin.

A loud knock on the door made her flinch. She got up, wrapped her flannel robe about her, and tied off the waist. Taking care to close the bedroom door behind her, she went to the door, grumbling, "Don't people know that I'm unemployed and sleep in in the mornings?"

"Good morning!" Avery's sometimes-too-cheerful smile greeted her. "I've weathered the storm and am now here to take you to breakfast."

"Why?"

Avery looked at Piper as though she'd lost it. "Because we had plans? Ugh, you forgot." She turned her head, rolling her eyes, but stopped at the sight of

Juan's jacket on the hook by the door. Suddenly suspicious, she said, "That looks familiar."

She turned to Piper and lifted an eyebrow, then she walked toward the fireplace and stared at the two whiskey glasses and the size-twelve shoes by the sofa. Slowly, she turned back to Piper, this time with both eyebrows lifted and an all-too-knowing tilt of the head.

Piper's mouth opened to offer an explanation. She just had to think of one. Then the master-suite shower turned on.

"Okay. I'm gonna go out on a limb and suggest you've got company now."

Piper nodded.

"Some guy with a jacket that looks remarkably like Juan's. What're the odds?"

Piper offered a guilty smile.

By now, Avery was beaming. She dragged Piper to the counter. "Sit down. Tell me everything. Hurry! Before he finishes his shower."

"No, not now. It's too new. Give us time to figure out what it is."

Avery smirked. "'What it is?'" She gave her head a slow shake and then pointed a finger first toward the bedroom and then at Piper. "What that is, is sex. And what this is, is you being crazy in love." She slammed her palms on the counter. "Oh my gosh, Piper, what happened?"

"What's going to happen is you're going to leave before he comes out and things get awkward. We're not ready for awkward. Not yet."

Avery couldn't seem to stop smiling. "Okay, okay. I'm outta here. Oh, Piper!" She gave her a hug. "We'll talk later."

Piper laughed. "Okay, sure."

Avery pointed a finger at Piper. "Oh, yes. We've got quite a talk in our future. And don't forget, you owe me a breakfast."

Just as they reached the door, Juan emerged from the bedroom with a towel wrapped around his waist. Seeing Avery, he stopped at the threshold.

"Morning, Juan. Good to see you!" She turned and practically sang, "See you soon, Piper."

She was gone before Juan got a word out.

Piper retrieved the two coffees from the kitchen counter. "In twenty minutes, the whole town will know."

Juan smiled as he took both coffees and set them back down. "That saves me the trouble of taking out that full-page ad I was planning." He grinned as he slid his hand down her arm and grasped her hand to lead her back into the bedroom.

EIGHT

Juan and Piper stood at the outskirts of the milling crowd at Pine Harbor's annual winter carnival, poring over the list of events.

"Hmm... let's see." Piper opened the brochure that listed the events, but something caught her eye on the donations page, and she laughed. "Look how they've classified donors this year: snowflakes, snowballs, snowpeople, and snow*banks*. Juan? Is that your name on the short list of snowbanks?"

He shrugged.

"But that's for donations of over... what?" She looked at him with wide eyes.

"I had a good year."

"I'll say."

He rolled his eyes and smiled uncomfortably.

"So, what's on the agenda for us?" He turned the page of her pamphlet.

She peered at him for a moment, with a half-dozen questions in mind that she couldn't ask him now. The man had neglected to mention he'd amassed a small fortune. "Well, I'm starving, so... food? Oh, here! Chili cook-off!"

"Excellent choice, madam. Right this way." He offered his arm, and they headed straight for the food tent.

Wasting no time, they both went through the line. Piper looked sideways at the two bowls in Juan's hands. With a mischievous grin, she said, "Hungry?"

He nodded shamelessly. She found herself feeling a bit jealous of how much he could eat and yet remain fit. Her mind flashed back to her bed where, hours ago, his sinewy body had been entwined with hers. Yes, he was better than fit.

"What's on your mind?"

Piper looked up at Juan, who was finishing his last spoonful of chili with unabashed enthusiasm.

"Oh, nothing. Well... maybe you." Their eyes met and lit with heart-bursting, eye-sparkling new love, even though it wasn't exactly new. But after so many years, it felt like it was.

Juan's mouth turned up at the corner. "Do I have a crazy-in-love, vomit-inducing grin on my face?"

"Yes." She laughed and shrugged.

"Good. I didn't want you to be alone."

They left the food tent, watched one heat of the snowshoe race, caught the juniors' figure-skating competition, passed up the long line for the sleigh ride, and settled by the warmth of the blazing bonfire. All the while, they ignored occasional and not always subtle looks from their friends and acquaintances. After a couple of hours, the cold got to Piper. "Let's go home and warm up."

Juan slid his arm around Piper's waist and pulled her close to whisper, "I think I can take care of that."

She looked at him, ready to toss a quip back to him, but the mood dissolved as she looked into his deep, dark brown eyes. "I lo—like you."

Juan laughed. "You like me? That's it?"

Piper stopped and looked at him. Too many emotions were swirling about, and she felt over-whelmed. "Let's not say it. Things are perfect right now."

His silent reaction unsettled her, but he nodded and walked her back to the lodge. She unlocked the door, and they both went inside. When their coats were hung up, Piper started to walk toward the kitchen. "Can I get you a coffee?"

Juan caught her hand and pulled her back into his arms. "I love you." Piper took a breath to speak, but he continued. "You may not want to hear it, but I've got to say it. I love you. And I'm not even sorry to say it."

She couldn't speak, so she nodded.

He looked worried and took hold of her shoulders. "Piper?" He shut his eyes and exhaled, then looked at her. "I should have listened to you and not said it."

She blurted out, "I love you too. I just don't want to jinx it."

His forehead creased. "I'll have to check the rule book, but I'm pretty sure love isn't jinxable."

Her eyes twinkled. "But you don't know for sure, do you?"

A smile teased his lips, but he grew serious. "It's too strong for that. At least, what I'm feeling is." He wrapped his arms around her and kissed her on the forehead. "It's stayed with me over the years, since those high school days when we used to meet in the library stacks."

She smiled and shrugged. "Maybe I was there for the books."

His eyes lit up as he drew her closer. "Oh, I know what you were there for." He leaned so close their lips nearly touched. "I think..." He kissed her forehead. "That you were there..." He kissed her on the cheek. "For this."

His lips brushed hers, but it was she who leaned closer and kissed him. He proceeded to make his point thoroughly and then leaned his forehead against hers. "I loved you then, and I've waited eight years to love you again. So I'm sorry, but I'm going to say it—and often."

"I don't know how you could, after the way I hurt you."

He looked into her eyes. "I'm not going to lie. It did hurt. But we were young, and it's in the past. It won't do us any good to dwell on it. We're here now, and that's all that matters."

Piper ran her fingers through her hair and stared into the fire. "I wish it could stay like this—perfect. But at some point, we're going to have to face real life."

"Your father?" Juan shook his head and put his hand on hers. "Piper, we're not those high school kids anymore. We're adults, and our lives are our own now."

She nodded, but she couldn't help feeling troubled.

"Come here." He held out his arms, and she nestled into his embrace. "We don't have to think or talk or plan. Let's just be together."

"Okay." She lifted her chin. "I do love you."

Juan's lips spread into a gentle smile. "You know,

for somebody who didn't want to say it, I keep hearing those words from you."

She averted her eyes. "I know. I've gone over the edge."

He frowned. "The edge of what?"

Piper shrugged. "I don't know. The edge of reason? The world? My comfort zone?"

"Well, let's see what we can do about that." He kissed her and made her forget all her worries as they spent the afternoon warmed by the fire and each other.

As Piper lay in Juan's arms and stared at the flames, she broached a subject that she'd wondered about all afternoon. "Juan, your donation..."

He sighed quietly. "I was expecting that." He shifted his position and sat facing her. "When you left, I was hurt." She looked up at him, but he shook his head. "I'm only bringing this up to explain what happened, not to make you feel guilty. You asked, so I'll tell you. For a long time, I was angry. I was so angry that I vowed I would never put myself in that position again.

"Your father was too tactful to say it to my face, but I knew why he didn't want you to marry me. And I knew money might have tipped the scale in my favor."

Piper remembered the night they told her

parents. Her father was quiet and deliberate. He sent Juan home and proceeded to reason with Piper. He used words like "those people" and "his sort." She'd have been a fool not to know what he meant, but he'd never spoken like that to Juan's face. He was just as concerned about money, and that was the only aspect Piper chose to share with Juan.

Juan's eyes narrowed. "He just assumed we were poor. We were never wealthy like you were, but my father worked hard and provided for us, and I would have worked hard and provided for you.

"Anyway, that's over now. The thing is—and this is something your father may never understand— we're proud people. I'm proud of who I am and of those who came before me. I wouldn't change it if I could. And back then, I knew how things were. I knew that your father wouldn't have minded my being Mexican half as much if I'd had money. So I worked. It wasn't as if I had anything else to do with my time.

"I poured myself into work. It was too late for us, but I was determined never to have to go through anything like that again. So I focused on the family business. I brought in new ways to manage our jobs, tracking labor and materials costs. My father didn't like computers, but he liked the results of what I could do with one, and he let me take over certain parts of the business. It paid off. It got to a point where my father thought he might retire and was ready to leave the business to me.

"Then my mother got sick. She went fast. A few weeks after the funeral, my father asked me to stay late on a work site to finish things up. When I got home, the house was empty. I went outside looking for him. The old fishing boat was gone. And then, I heard a gunshot."

Piper leaned forward and put her hand on his. "I'm so sorry."

He nodded without looking at her. "After that, I couldn't get busy enough, so I went to college online. I started playing the stock market with my inheritance, and I made some lucky investments. All those years, I just wanted to prove I was as good as anyone else. And then one day, I realized nobody cared, or maybe I didn't care. I don't know. I just knew that it didn't make me feel better about myself, so I stopped trying to prove myself, and I started helping others instead."

"Juan..."

"No, let me finish. You know I've never liked talking about myself, so I need to get this all out so I won't have to talk about it again."

Piper nodded. He probably hadn't shared this with anyone else before now. As many friends as he had, none of them were close enough for him to confide in—not like she and Avery did.

Juan stared at the fire. "At some point, I began to feel nearly normal. Then you came home, and the old feelings came back—not the good ones, but the pain. I wanted to hate you, and I did my best. But you're still you. You've grown up, but you're still the same Piper I loved. And I couldn't help what happened."

"What do you mean?"

He turned to face her. "I fell back in love." He squeezed her hand and said, "Back to the money... I'm not rich, so don't get too excited." He smiled. "But I have a safety net. It makes me feel secure, so I'm glad that I have it. But I don't want it—or my desire for it—to rule my life or ours."

Piper hooked her arm into his. "The only desire I have right now is for you, so come here." She rested her head on his shoulders and, for the first time since high school, felt that once-familiar and since longed-for connection.

NINE

Juan and Piper sat in the back of the balcony of the
Pine Harbor Movie House, huddled together over a
shared bag of popcorn. Originally a vaudeville
theater, the old building had evolved with the passing
times to become a regular stop on the old straw-hat
circuit of summer stock theaters. In its heyday, live
touring shows came through town and entertained
summer tourists. But with the advent of multiplex
theaters and cable TV, it fell on hard times and eventually closed its tattered curtain in the eighties.

More than a decade later, determined town resi-
dents with a vision worked with dogged determina-
tion to raise funds to refurbish and reopen it. Its
vintage charm was now a source of local pride. On
this evening, it was a venue for one of the evening
events of the town's winter carnival. Tonight's film

was an old black-and-white movie called *Portrait of Jennie.*

As the ending credits rolled, Juan looked over at Piper, who was dabbing her eyes with a tissue. He smiled, put his arm around her, and pulled her close to him. "Crashing waves got to you?"

She looked up at him. "Don't make fun of me."

"I'm sorry. It really did get to you, didn't it?"

She glanced at him, slightly annoyed. "'The strands of our lives are woven together?' Two people in love who are separated but find one another across the boundaries of time? Yeah, it's completely unre-latable."

"Point taken. But the difference is we're not ghosts, and we don't have that annoying music playing all the time in the background."

Piper looked at him as if he'd just kicked a puppy. "That 'annoying music' is Debussy."

"Good to know. If it shows up on a playlist, I'll be sure to delete it."

She shut her eyes and shook her head slowly.

The houselights were cranked up to the blind-ingly bright setting. Piper put her tissue back in her pocket. "I think they're trying to tell us something."

As they headed downstairs, Juan took Piper's elbow and held her back for a moment. He muttered,

"Don't look now, but your old boyfriend's down there."

"He's not my old boyfriend."

"It's not like he didn't try hard enough." Juan studied the woman in Grayson's clutches. "I'll say one thing for him, the dude gets around."

Piper shrugged. "I can't say I'm surprised. There's something about him. Just a little too charming. And he hurt Avery, so he's dead to me."

"Good. I like a happy ending. Now, let's get over to the Harbor House Bar before they run out of beer."

"I could text Avery to hoard a few bottles for us. But seriously, I could have her put in our order."

"Wow, thirsty but efficient! Have I ever told you I love you? Wait, you're not really putting in our drink order, are you?"

Piper laughed and glanced up from her cell phone. "No, I'm telling her we're on our way." As they stepped outside, Piper looked up from her phone. "It's snowing. Again." She pulled her hood up. "I think this might be more snow than we had all last year."

The bar was packed, but Avery was valiantly saving their seats. Piper sat down while Juan went to get them some drinks.

"Look who's just arrived."

Piper followed Avery's eye roll, which led her to Grayson, who hovered possessively over his date as they leaned against the wall in the corner.

Avery fidgeted with her cocktail napkin. "I shouldn't care. He's a jerk. But the heart wants what the heart wants."

Piper measured her words. "Why does the heart want to be with a jerk?"

Avery began tearing her napkin into tiny pieces. "Because all men are jerks, and because, jerk or not, he wanted to be with me, at least for a couple of days, and I liked it."

Piper sighed. "Avery, he's done you a favor. You deserve someone who's good to you and who makes you feel special."

Avery wasn't buying it, but she nodded.

Juan arrived with their drinks. In contrast to Avery's mood, the bar atmosphere was especially lively, no doubt due to the winter carnival crowd. The bar had hired a DJ for the event, and people were starting to dance.

While Avery stared at her drink, Juan turned to Piper. "C'mon."

She shook her head slightly and cast a sympathetic glance at her friend. Juan picked up the cue and asked Avery to dance. When she shook her head, Piper looked at the area now serving as a dance floor.

It was a fast dance, and people were dancing in groups, so Piper dragged Avery along, and the three of them danced. Before long, Avery forgot not to smile.

After dancing five dances in a row, Avery said that she needed to go. She had work in the morning. "Thanks, Pipes. I feel better."

They hugged.

"I'll walk you to your car." Juan turned to Piper. "I'll be right back."

"Actually, I wouldn't mind heading for home."

A mischievous glint came to Juan's eyes. Piper smiled. As they walked to the parking lot in back, Juan asked, "You're okay to drive, aren't you?"

Avery pulled out her keys. "Oh, yeah. I just had the one beer an hour ago, and I've danced it all off, so I'm fine."

The three said their goodbyes, and Avery pulled out of the lot. Juan turned to Piper and pulled her into his arms. "So, you wanted to go home early. Just what did you have in mind?"

Piper lifted her eyes to meet his. "I don't know. But I've got some ideas."

He nuzzled closer. "I've got some ideas too." He kissed her.

The sound of a skidding car cut through the night air, followed by the thud of metal on metal, and then the hissing of steam. Juan took Piper's hand, and they ran toward the sound.

A car was turned around, facing oncoming traffic. Other cars managed to stop just in time. Avery's car sat askew in the middle of the road, airbag exploded, and Avery's head was against the window, not moving. Someone started to open Avery's car door.

"No!" Juan grabbed the man's arm and stopped him. "Wait for the paramedics. Her neck might be injured."

Piper called 911, but she heard sirens as she dialed the call, so someone else must have called it in first. There were extra police on duty for the winter carnival, so they didn't have far to go.

A man staggered out of the other car. Someone asked if he was okay. He said he was, but he tripped and fell to the curb, where he sat looking disoriented. A police car arrived on the scene.

The next few minutes seemed like forever, but an ambulance finally arrived. Avery moaned as they pulled her from her car and put her in the ambulance. Juan and Piper watched it drive off, and they headed home to get Juan's truck and go to the hospital.

They walked past the other driver as the paramedics finished examining him. One of the officers said something about blood-alcohol level as they led him to their patrol car.

TWO HOURS LATER, Piper was draped over Juan, dozing off in a waiting-room chair. A nurse approached and told them they could see Avery at last. She had suffered a concussion, and they were keeping her overnight for observation.

They walked into the room to find Avery looking doe-eyed at her broad-shouldered male nurse as he fluffed up her pillows. "I'll be back in an hour. Don't go anywhere." He smiled at Avery and turned to greet Piper and Juan as he left the room.

Avery watched the nurse walk away. When he rounded the corner to go down the hall, Avery muttered to Piper, "Like I'd go anywhere knowing he's coming back. Did you get a look at him?"

Piper rested her hands on the bed rail. "Yes, I did. Please tell me you didn't get into an accident just to meet a good-looking nurse."

"No, but if I'd known he was waiting at the other end of an ambulance ride, I might have considered it."

Piper's eyes sparkled. "I guess he's okay, if you like that type."

"Sandy-blond hair, kind eyes, muscular shoulders, great ass? Yeah, who wouldn't like that type?"

Juan watched the exchange with an amused smirk. "Someone's feeling better."

"Well, my head hurts, but I'm trying not to think about it."

He nodded. "You're doing an excellent job."

The three talked and watched TV for an hour until Avery's parents arrived. Piper and Juan took that as their cue to leave with a promise to return the next day.

TEN

It was nearly noon when a loud knock sounded at the door. Piper opened one eye and looked at the clock. "I don't think I've slept this late since my college pro-sleeping days."

Juan sat up. The knock sounded again. "Are you going to answer that?"

Piper groaned. "Eventually." She got up and threw on her robe. Juan went commando, pulling his jeans up and putting on a T-shirt. He was on his way to the kitchen for coffee when Piper opened the door.

"Daddy! Lainey!"

"Piper... Juan?"

Several moments of silence and ricocheted glances came next before Piper recovered.

"Hadley." Juan reached out his hand and did his

best to summon a winning smile, which was more than he could say for Piper's father. But under the circumstances, Juan considered himself lucky that a blank stare was the worst he got.

Piper took a step back. "Come in."

Her parents walked in and sat down on the sofa.

"Can I get you some coffee?"

"I'll get it." Juan volunteered a little too quickly and left for the kitchen.

Piper sat on the edge of the chair facing her father and stepmother. "So... you're here."

Lainey Harriman was a petite woman with a blond ponytail and a face untroubled by thought. "Didn't you get our emails?"

Piper shook her head. "I've been kind of busy."

Lainey glanced over at Juan, who was busy making coffee.

Piper followed Lainey's eyes and ignored her raised eyebrow. "Why didn't you call to let me know you were coming?"

Before she could answer, Juan arrived with the coffee. Once everyone was served, he pulled up a chair beside Piper.

Hadley Harriman looked past Piper and Juan to the rumpled bedclothes in the bedroom, and then back at Piper.

Piper got straight to the point. "We're together now, Daddy."

Her father took a moment to consider. "Well, we're not here to talk about that."

Piper leaned forward. "I'm sorry, but I think that we should."

Juan leaned close and said softly, "This might not be the best time."

Piper leaned forward emphatically. "After eight years, I don't think there's going to be a better time." She straightened her posture and drew in a breath. "We're back together, and we're still in love." Lainey tried to interrupt, but Piper continued. "So that's that."

Juan gave Piper a cautious glance, then leaned his elbows on his knees. "Hadley, I'm sorry. I know this is a surprise."

"Daddy, I'm twenty-six years old. You can't stop me from doing what I want to do."

Piper's father glanced at her, then met Juan's gaze directly. "Juan, you and I have known each other for a long time. We've done business together. I've seen how you've managed yourself and your business. You've done a good job, and I respect you. But Piper's my daughter. I want the best for her."

"And I'll see that she has it." Juan clenched his jaw.

With a skeptical nod, Hadley looked straight at Juan, and then turned softer eyes to his daughter. "Well, that's not why I'm here. I've got something to tell you."

Something in her father's expression alarmed Piper.

Hadley said, "Juan, you may as well stay for this, but what I'm about to tell you cannot go outside of this house."

Juan nodded.

"Some investments have gone bad. I've lost nearly everything."

Piper exhaled and grabbed Juan's hand. "Oh, thank God. I thought you were sick. Oh my gosh, it's just money."

Hadley's eyes widened. "A lot of money. We're going to have to sell the house, and that includes the Winter Lodge too. We've come up to meet with a real-estate agent, and we're pricing to sell, so we're expecting to settle this fast."

"But you can't sell our home! This is where I grew up. It's been in our family for generations."

Hadley snapped at Piper, "We don't have a choice!"

"I don't understand."

"You don't have to." Hadley looked worn.

Juan squeezed Piper's hand, but she barely

noticed. She'd never imagined losing their family home.

Juan turned to Hadley. "Why don't you stay in your home while you're here?"

"But that's your home right now. You've paid your rent, Juan."

Piper couldn't help but be struck by how civil Hadley was being toward Juan. She could only assume that her father was so overwhelmed by his financial problems that Piper and Juan were the least of his concerns, at least for now.

Juan insisted, "I'll stay here in the lodge. The house is all yours."

Without waiting for her husband, Lainey said, "Thank you. We'd love to."

Hadley didn't look thrilled. After all, this would mean Juan would stay here with his daughter. But he agreed to the arrangement.

AVERY WAS SITTING UP, watching a reality TV show, when Piper and Juan arrived at her hospital room.

Piper set a plant down on the window ledge. "So, how's our patient?"

"I'm fine, but the doctor wants to keep me one

more night, just to make sure that the bleeding's subsided."

"Bleeding?"

"Just a little." Avery looked perfectly chipper as she sipped water through a bendy straw.

"Just a little bleeding?" Piper made no effort to hide her shock.

"The doctor said a small amount showed up on the CT scan, so they're keeping me one more night for observation. She seems to think I'll be able to go home in the morning."

Piper nodded, brow furrowed. "Do you have a ride home?"

"My mom said she'd come get me."

Juan said, "If that changes, call us. We'd be happy to come get you."

Piper nodded in agreement and frowned. "It's too bad you're stuck here one more night, though."

Avery's eyes brightened. "Oh, I don't mind too much."

Piper's face wrinkled up as she scrutinized Avery. "What do you mean you don't mind? Everybody minds being in the hospital."

Avery's eyes sparkled. "Not everybody has Nurse Noah."

Piper knew she was missing some facts. "Wait, was Nurse Noah the nurse we saw yesterday?"

Avery's eyes sparkled. "Mm-hmm." She leaned closer to Piper and spoke softly. "He has to come check on me every hour through the night to make sure I haven't slipped into a coma."

Piper eyed her. "Oh, that must be horrible for you."

Avery smiled. "Having a hottie stopping by every hour to take care of my every need? Well, maybe not *every* need, but yes, it's been trying. By which I mean, I'll be *trying* to get his phone number." She suddenly lowered her voice. "Oh, there he is!" They watched him walk past the wall-to-wall window, then Piper turned back to her friend.

Avery lifted her eyebrows. "I know. I'm the luckiest girl in the world."

Juan eyed her. "Getting hit by a drunk driver isn't exactly what I'd call lucky."

"Glass half empty, eh Juan? I like to think of it as God's little consolation prize." Avery grinned.

"So, how's my favorite patient?" asked Nurse Noah. "Time to check your vitals."

Avery glanced at Piper and lifted an eyebrow. Piper smiled and said, "We'll see you tomorrow."

Juan waved and took Piper's hand, leaving behind the happiest patient in Pine Harbor Hospital.

THE HARBOR WAS FROZEN in stark whites and grays that stretched out to a cloudy gray horizon. Piper and Juan sat in a waterside restaurant across from Piper's father and stepmother. They'd already ordered, and the conversation had found its way back to Hadley's investment debacle.

Lainey said, "His new financial advisor managed a hedge fund. All of his friends who'd invested in it were making boatloads of money, and we wanted in."

Juan tried not to frown. "How did you know it was doing so well?"

"Because he told us. And he was doing so well." Lainey was so earnest, she almost seemed to believe in him still.

Hadley said, "The guy was dripping with money —nice watch, sleek little sports car. He knew some people I knew."

"So you dumped Margate and Strong." Piper turned to Juan and said, "His old brokerage firm."

Hadley winced. "Their expense ratios were brutal. I'd been meaning to move at least some of my money, so it seemed like fate to get paired with this financial genius."

"They were paired for a round on the golf course." Lainey leaned forward, explaining.

Juan clenched his jaw. The man had moved a

small fortune based on advice from a guy he'd just met on a golf course.

"I know what you must be thinking." Hadley looked from Juan to Piper. "But I'd known him for months before I decided to invest."

"Two months." Lainey took a sip and set down her water glass.

"Investing is never a sure thing. I took a chance, and I lost."

"What's his name?"

"Grayson Endicott."

Juan and Piper exchanged glances.

Hadley's eyes widened. "You know him?"

Piper nodded. "We've met." She cast another look at Juan as the food arrived and remained unusually quiet for the rest of the meal.

AS JUAN PULLED into the driveway and parked, Piper said, "I need to run out to the store."

"Why didn't you say something? We could have stopped on the way home."

Piper shrugged. "I forgot."

"Forgot what?"

She gave him a perturbed look. "Lady products. I'll be back in a few."

She hopped out of his truck and into her car before he could say more, and she was off. Minutes later, she pulled into the driveway of the blue house at the end of the lake. Avery had mentioned it once or twice, so she knew exactly where to go. Grayson was renting this house until he could find one of his own. She got out of her car and went up to the front door. After ringing the bell three times, he finally answered the door. A woman's shoe and a purse lay on the floor halfway down the hall. Beyond that was a scarf.

"Piper." He raked his hand through his hair with a confused expression on his face. "It's great to see you, but..." He looked behind him. "I, uh, can't really talk now."

"Good, 'cause I've got plenty to say for the both of us."

Piper was fuming, yet Grayson looked entirely unruffled. It seemed as though he'd been through this before.

"What sort of scam are you running? You've practically ruined my father. And don't think I'll just let that go. I don't know what's going on with you, but I will. And I promise you'll pay."

Grayson took a step back and began to close the door. Piper put her foot in the way. "Oh, and one more thing." She punched him in the face and got back in her car and drove off.

Juan was sitting at the counter, arms folded, when she returned home. "No shopping bag?"

From one look at his face, Piper knew there was no use hiding the truth. She shook her head.

Juan's expression hardened. "The phone rang. I thought your parents might need something at the house, so I picked up. It was Grayson—with a few choice things to say about sending a woman to do a man's work."

Piper bristled. "I had to."

"Did you have to risk your life too? Going alone? He could have had a gun. You don't know. I could have gone with you."

"I doubt you're any more impervious to gunfire than I am. But I appreciate the chivalry. It's sweet." She moved toward him, expecting an embrace, but instead she got wrath like she'd never seen from Juan.

"I am not being sweet!" He looked about and exhaled. "God, Piper, you're not a superhero. If your dad screwed up—and we both know he did—punching Grayson is not going to fix it."

"Maybe not, but it made me feel better." She went to the freezer, pulled out a package of peas, and held it against her knuckles.

"Come here. Let me see." He examined her knuckles. "Look at you. A one-woman force to be reckoned with." He lifted his eyes and said softly, "After he unloaded every curse word he knew, he told me he's going to file a police report."

She couldn't meet his eyes, so she went to the sofa and sat. Alone.

Minutes of silence stretched out between them before Juan came and sat down beside her.

"It's my home, Juan. Grayson lost it. It's been in our family—"

"I know. Generations. But you've only been in it for one, and you mean something to me. More than that stack of old lumber."

"And memories." She looked at him.

His manner softened. "The memories haven't gone anywhere, have they?"

"No, but..."

"But let's see if we can't find a way that's safer— and one that will hurt him a lot more than whatever you said or did."

"Oh, I hurt him."

"Did you?" A smile teased at his mouth.

"I bloodied his nose." A proud smile bloomed on her face but dissolved to a pout. "But my hand hurts like you wouldn't believe."

"Give me that." Juan took her hand and kissed each knuckle.

Piper smiled. "Avery's not the only one with a good-looking nurse."

ELEVEN

The next morning, Piper and Juan took Avery home from the hospital and returned to find Hadley walking the property with his real-estate agent and the home inspector he'd hired. Juan and Piper waved and started toward the lodge, but Hadley flagged them down.

"Juan, I could use your expertise." They proceeded to talk about some repairs and improvements that needed to be done before the house could be put on the market. The agent headed off to his office to put together the listing. Juan agreed to do the repairs and renovations, so he went off with the inspector to further discuss the recommended changes.

Piper stood next to her father and watched Juan as he pointed and talked. He was not that much different from the tall, muscular boy she'd fallen for years ago. "I love him, Daddy."

Hadley was quiet for a moment. "I suppose you're still angry with me." She looked into his eyes, and he added, "For keeping you two apart?"

Piper said nothing.

"Was it so wrong for me to want the best for my baby girl?"

"It was wrong to want *your* best when *my* best was Juan."

He nodded as if conceding her point. "But do you really regret going to college?"

"No. I wanted that too. But I loved him. Nothing's changed there. I still love him."

"You know, I don't have anything against him."

"That's not what you said eight years ago."

"I've always liked Juan. He's done a lot of work for me over the years, and I've come to like and respect him."

Piper leveled a look. "As the hired help."

Hadley returned Piper's pointed gaze. "That's not fair. You were both young and fresh out of high school. You were in no position to start a life together."

Piper stared off toward the sea. "You know, I've always wondered how you would have reacted if I'd come home wanting to marry someone more like your golf buddy, Grayson Endicott. Proper pedigree, travels in the right circles..."

Hadley said, "You can't tell me money doesn't make a difference."

"No, I can't. But I can tell you Grayson's a complete jerk."

"Being financially comfortable matters."

"Yes, it's nice, but given the choice between comfort and character, I'll choose character."

Her father's expression gave nothing away. "And Juan has that?"

"Yes."

"Well, good."

"But...?" Piper didn't want to hear it, but she needed him to admit it."

Hadley's eyes burned with annoyance. "You're trying to put words in my mouth."

"Only the ones you're thinking." She lifted her chin and looked at him plainly. "What you meant to say was that he's a good man... for a Mexican."

Hadley shook his head emphatically. "For anyone else but my daughter."

Piper looked down and spoke softly. "I was hoping you'd changed."

"You're a grown woman. I won't stand in your way."

"Because you can't, and you know it." Piper's anger turned to sadness.

The angry edge in Hadley's voice cut through the air. "What do you want from me, Piper?"

"Your blessing? Juan asked for it once. He won't ask you again, but I'd like it."

Hadley could not meet her eyes. "I don't know what good that would do. You're already shacking up with him. What difference does it make?"

"After waiting eight years? Yeah, I guess we are shacking up."

Piper looked away. She was wasting her time. There was no more to say. There were things about her father that would never change. He had always been stubborn, but now that this financial situation had broken his spirit, there was no reasoning with him. His head was too cluttered with worries and pain to get past it and open himself to new ways of thinking. He was only a bitter and broken man.

Hadley heaved a deep sigh. "Go ahead. Do what you want, and get married." With a shrug, he added, "I'll go to the wedding."

That wasn't exactly the wholehearted blessing she'd hoped for, but she supposed it was all she was going to get. If eight years hadn't taught her, maybe now it was time to accept how things were without hoping for more.

"Oh, there's one more thing, Daddy. Juan hasn't asked me to marry him yet, so let's not mention a wedding to him, okay?"

He turned slowly to look at her. "Piper?"

"Yes?" She wasn't sure she wanted to hear any more.

"You're just like your mother." And then Hadley did something that completely surprised and confused Piper. He smiled.

Her father rarely mentioned her mother. She'd died when Piper was so young that she had only a few faded memories of her. But when her father said this, she was gripped by emotion.

Juan finished with the home inspector and came over to discuss plans with Hadley. To his credit, Hadley behaved as though all were well between them. They firmed up plans for the work on the house, and the four of them went out to dinner at Hadley and Lainey's favorite seafood restaurant. Perhaps it was the wine, but a bit of the tension had eased, and a glimmer of hope worked its way into Piper's heart.

PIPER HUNG her coat on the hook by the door of the lodge. "You and my father were yucking it up."

Juan wrinkled his face and looked baffled. "He was telling some jokes."

"How do you do it?"

"Do what?"

"Smile and laugh at his jokes when he's treated you badly."

"Because that was a long time ago. I've grown up, and he doesn't have that sort of power over me anymore."

"Why not?"

"Because I won't give it to him."

"But doesn't it bother you?"

"There's a lot that bothers me from the past. Losing you, mainly. But anger's a heavy burden to carry around all your life. We're together now, and I'd rather let go of the rest and focus on you." His eyes shone as he looked at her and smiled. "Because you make me happy. And I hope I can return the favor." He drew her into his arms and kissed her.

Piper whispered, "That's a good start." She kissed him again. "Are you tired?"

"No."

"Good. Let's go to bed."

JUAN PULLED the car over to the curb of the airport passenger drop-off and pulled Hadley and Lainey's suitcases from the trunk of the car. Piper hugged her father and stepmother, Juan shook their hands, and the two went inside to catch their flight back to Florida.

As they got back in the car and headed for home, Piper said, "When does the work begin on the house?"

"I'll start work in the morning, and I've got a crew lined up for the afternoon. It shouldn't take us more than a week."

"And then the agent will start showing the house?"

"That's the plan."

"Isn't that going to be inconvenient for you?"

Juan glanced at her. "Well, I was going to talk to you about that. Would you mind if I stayed at the lodge with you?"

Piper grinned. "I think we can work something out." Her grin faded.

"What?"

"I didn't say anything."

"No, but I can hear you thinking from here."

Piper hesitated. "Well, I was thinking as soon as the house sells, I'll be losing my home. I guess I'd better start looking."

He glanced at her and put his hand on hers. "Don't worry."

"Easy for you to say. Wait. Your house isn't finished, so you'll be homeless too."

He looked unperturbed. "I've got something in mind."

"Good for you, but I don't."

He sighed and shook his head. "Piper Harriman, trust me. I'll take care of it."

While Piper did trust him, she was a numbers and columns kind of girl. She liked things she could count and things she could count on, so this went against everything she believed in.

"Take care of what?" She couldn't take the not knowing, especially since she was sure he knew how frustrating this was for her.

A gentle look came into his eyes. "I love you. I will always love you. And I'll take care of you. Please don't ask me for more. Not right this moment." He squeezed her hand, and somehow, her nagging need to make plans was overshadowed by her heart, which was so full of love.

PIPER SPENT the next morning poring over her father's investments. She'd offered to see if she could reallocate his investments to better advantage. But she was also trying to figure out what had happened to her father's wealth.

For the past year, Grayson had managed Hadley's investments. It didn't take long to discover that Grayson had moved the majority of Hadley's funds about like some sort of securities shell game. In the process, her father had incurred a large amount of capital gains, which had tax implications her father would still have to face.

After six months of shifting money around, the majority of it seemed to have ended up in a fund managed by a company Piper had never heard of called the Endicott Group. Aside from the losses, something didn't look right, but she couldn't seem to pinpoint it.

She found Juan in the house with his crew. They were tearing up carpet and preparing to replace it with hardwood. She stood, car keys in hand. "I'm going out for a while. I'll be back in a couple of hours."

"Okay. Where?"

"I need to see Avery."

"She's not working?"

"She is. That's why I need to see her."

"Okay." He returned to his work.

Fifteen minutes later, Piper walked into the

District Attorney's office where Avery worked as a paralegal.

"Piper! Did I forget something? Were we meeting for lunch?"

"No, but we could. Actually, that would be perfect. When's your lunch break?"

"I might be able to take my lunch early. Hold on." She returned moments later with her coat and purse on her arm. "Okay, let's go."

They walked to a quiet café. When they were seated, Piper pulled out a file and held it for a moment. "This is absolutely confidential."

"What is it, your diary?" Piper started to smile, but it dissolved when she saw Piper's somber reaction.

"This is a printout of my father's investments. Our friend Grayson has been very busy."

Avery frowned. "Grayson? How so?"

Piper opened the file on the table and filled Avery in on the overall picture, then went through document by document, pointing out some specifics.

"I think something's wrong here. I don't really know much about this sort of thing, but it looks as though it might be some sort of investment scam. Do you know anyone who could help us with this?"

Avery narrowed her eyes. "That's funny. When Grayson and I were together—during that brief delusional episode I had—he asked me about money more than once. He was pretty smooth, asking whether I owned my house and what sort of salary a paralegal makes. He told me he was curious because his sister was thinking of becoming one, but looking back, he got a pretty good picture of my financial situation. And that's when he dumped me—as soon as he realized I didn't have money. That bastard! He was never interested in me. Now I'm mad! Let me at him!"

"Get in line behind me. He lost my father's retirement nest egg, so I'm just as mad."

Avery gripped the file folder. "If this is some sort of securities fraud, I might know some people who could help you with this. May I take this?"

Piper nodded. "Please do."

"If it's what we're thinking, I don't think our office would handle it. It might be a federal matter, but I've got some friends."

An hour later, Piper was on her way home, worrying about the file landing on somebody's desk only to languish in the low-priority pile. She had had occasion, through work, to see some of those federal government offices with stacks of files on desks and tables, waiting months to be dealt with.

She couldn't wait for them to get around to her father's. And besides, she had nothing but time. Juan was busy with work on the house. If she did some of the legwork, she might speed things along. It might be too late to save her father's house, but she might get back some of his money. At the very least, she intended to make Grayson pay. If he couldn't pay back the cash, then prison time would do.

Back at home, Piper scanned every online resource she could find for any information about Grayson's company. The investment documents and correspondence listed an Endicott Group in Manhattan. She called it and got a receptionist, who asked if she'd like to leave a message. That was the last thing Piper needed to do, so she hung up and dug deeper.

As darkness fell, she had drilled down far enough to have found several flags that raised serious doubts about the Endicott Group. What she had so far was still inconclusive, but she emailed it to Avery and asked her to share it with her contacts in law enforcement, in the hope that they could get the evidence to investigate Grayson for fraud.

As she pressed the Send key, Juan walked in the door. "Hi, honey. I'm home!"

Piper laughed. "You sound good saying that."

"Yeah? Well, you look good sitting there." He sauntered over and planted a kiss on Piper's cheek. "This is so much better than how I usually end my work days."

Her eyes shone. "My day's not looking bad, either."

Juan took her hands and drew her to her feet and into his arms. "Come here, you. Let's see what we can do to make it even better." He nuzzled his way up her neck and kissed her just under her ear, while he cradled the back of her head with his hand. He was working his other hand up from her waist when a knock at the door interrupted his progress.

Piper exhaled her frustration and winced. "I'll get it."

Juan gripped her hand and pulled her back his arms. His gaze darkened. "Remember where we left off. I'm not finished with you."

She met his gaze and put her palm on his chest. "Good. Hold that thought."

She pulled open the door to find two police officers. "Piper Harriman?"

She lifted her eyebrows. "Yes?"

The male officer said, "We've got a warrant for your arrest. We need you to come with us to the station."

"You can't be serious."

Juan stepped forward.

"Stay there, sir," said the male officer.

His partner turned to Piper and proceeded to put

handcuffs on her. "We're arresting you for assault. You have the right to remain silent."

Piper strained her neck to look back at Juan.

"Anything you say can and will be used against you..." The officer continued reciting the Miranda rights as she escorted Piper to the patrol car.

Juan called after her, "I'll be right behind you, Piper. Don't worry. We'll sort this mess out."

She was put into the back of the patrol car, and they took her away.

TWELVE

Piper retrieved her personal effects and walked through a door in the police station. Juan was waiting there for her. She flew into his arms.

"Let's get out of here, babe."

She breathed in. "You smell so good."

As the police station door closed behind them, Piper said, "He actually did it. That bastard, Grayson." Juan put an arm about her waist, and they walked down the steps. "Thanks for bailing me out. Wow. Words I never expected to say. At least my father wasn't here to see this proud moment."

"He missed it by one day."

Piper frowned. "I guess I'll have to tell him at some point."

"Like tomorrow? We're picking them up at the airport. Remember?"

Piper sighed. "I'll think about that tomorrow."

Juan pulled out his keys and unlocked the car. "What I can't understand is what took Grayson so long. You punched him yesterday. I thought maybe he'd file something in civil court, maybe get a restraining order just to scare you, but criminal charges? That's a little excessive."

Deep in thought, Piper got into Juan's truck. Once he was seated inside, Juan turned to Piper. "What aren't you telling me?"

She lifted her eyes to meet his penetrating stare. "I have a theory."

He shut his eyes and leaned back against the head rest. "If Grayson were going to do something out of anger, he'd have done it last night. But he didn't. Instead, he waited for nearly twenty-four hours. Something happened today. What was it?"

"I don't know how this could be connected, but you know how I thought there might be something funny about those investments Grayson talked my father into making?"

"Yeah."

"Turns out, Avery knows someone who might be able to help, so she gave her the file."

"That's it? Good. Now we wait."

Piper sucked air through her teeth. "Not exactly. At least I didn't wait. Look, can we talk somewhere besides the police station parking lot? I've spent enough time here for one day."

Juan had always grown quiet when he was angry, but his flared nostrils and clenched jaw were a new level of anger. He put the truck in gear and drove home in silence.

As soon as they walked inside, Piper confessed, "I made a phone call."

"To?"

"The Endicott Group."

"As in Grayson Endicott?" Juan rolled his eyes.

"Before you say anything, I didn't give my name. I didn't even ask anything very specific to arouse suspicion."

"Caller ID."

"They didn't accept blocked calls, so I figured they must get dozens of calls every day. Why would mine stand out?"

"It wouldn't. Unless Grayson has something to hide, and he got wind of your sniffing around his business affairs."

"Which brings us back to the phone call. There's no way—unless he reads his phone records at night as a sleep aid."

"Piper, he could have his company phone records searched.

And there you are, with your 207 area code."

Piper winced and rubbed her temples.

"Or, forget the phone call. The guy's well-connected. All it takes is one crony—a golf buddy—to see a file on a desk with his name attached. He makes a quick call to alert him."

"Oh crap."

Juan nodded. "That pretty well sums it up."

"Oh crap!" Piper stared at the floor, shaking her head.

"I believe we've established that."

Piper groaned. "So to push back, he filed the assault charges."

"Did you admit anything to the police officers?"

"No. Excuse me, you're looking at a *Law and Order* binge watcher here. I've picked up some pointers."

"Good. We'll get you a lawyer."

She said weakly, "Maybe there are no witnesses, and this will just go away."

"Piper. It's the twenty-first century. If there aren't witnesses, there are cameras. His rental house might have security cameras all over the place." Juan ran his fingers through his hair. "Anyway, let's worry about that later. Let's focus on getting a good lawyer, and we'll get through this. But, Piper?"

She took a break from frowning and looked into his eyes.

"Don't do anything. Just let the professionals take it from here."

She found his instructive tone a bit condescending. "What would I do?"

"I don't know. I have visions of you and Avery going on some sort of Lucy and Ethel caper. Stay clear of his house and his business. If you violate that protection-from-harassment order, they might not let me bail you out again."

Piper sighed. "I forgot about the restraining order."

"Well, remember, because he will."

She wasn't about to disagree, but she wasn't happy about it.

A LIGHT DUSTING of snow overnight freshened up the wintry look of the town, leaving it looking clean and untroubled. Juan and Piper were headed for a dinner out the next evening to help get Piper's mind off her problems. He told her they needed to make a stop on the way. Ten minutes up the coast, Juan turned off the main road to a small private road that wound its way through pine trees. He came to a stop, took out his phone, and pressed something that lit up the house.

"Juan, what is this? It's gorgeous. But—"

"Wait. Don't move." With a satisfied grin, he got out of the truck, came around to her side, and opened the door.

She took his hand and stepped down to the ground. "You're very fancy this evening."

He smiled and led her by the hand toward the house. There was just enough light to make out the silhouette of treetops against the starry night sky. A clear path led down to the water, where a few lights could be seen along the curve of the shoreline.

Piper said, "This reminds me of the place we used to go. Remember? A developer had laid down the road but run out of money before building a housing community. Wait, is this it?" She looked at him with wonder.

"It is."

"Juan?"

"Shh. Follow me." They went to the back of the house and climbed up the steps of a large porch that looked out to the sea.

"Are you sure we should be doing this? The last thing I need is to be arrested for trespassing."

"Don't worry. You won't. I know the owner." He smiled.

Piper took in a breath. "This is just how we dreamed it. Remember? A large house, not too modern, but with a clean design and a wall of windows." She turned around and looked up at windows with warm light spilling through them.

Juan watched her reaction with a satisfied smile. "Let's go inside."

"Great. We can add breaking and entering to my rap sheet."

He pulled out his phone and unlocked the door. Piper's face lit up. "Oh. Is this one of your jobs? Well, it's gorgeous!"

He nodded. "It's a pet project, of sorts."

She looked around at the massive great room with the two-story wall of windows behind a large stone fireplace to the right, and a state-of-the-art kitchen to the left. "Oh wow! This is amazing!"

He couldn't help it. He knew he was beaming. He'd worked and hoped for just such a reaction. As he touched his phone to turn on the gas fireplace, he said, "It was supposed to be finished by now, but I got busy with other projects."

"My father's house."

He reluctantly nodded.

"Well, even so, the homeowner must be thrilled with this."

"He is now."

She turned with a sudden realization. "Juan, it's not yours!"

"Well, I know the timing sucks, but I can't wait. We'll both be homeless soon, so I thought—I was hoping that this might be ours—that you'd live here with me."

"I'm stunned. We used to dream about a place like this."

"I know. That's why I built it."

He dropped on one knee. Piper gasped.

"I never thought I'd have the chance to ask you again." He reached into his pocket and pulled out a small box.

Piper's hands flew to her mouth, and he couldn't help but smile at her reaction. "Piper Harriman—"

"Yes!"

"Let me finish. Piper Harriman, you are my first and my only love. Will you marry me?"

"Yes!"

He put the emerald ring on her finger and stood up to receive quite a payoff for his efforts. Some tears were included, but after so many years, he could understand why.

"So you like it?"

"Like what? The gorgeous ring, the spectacular house, and the most amazing man in the world?" Her eyes sparkled. "Yes, I do. I like all of the above."

He pressed his lips to hers and held her against him. "I love you," he murmured as he kissed her again. The warm light from the fire mixed with the soft lights in the room to make the moment as perfect as he'd hoped it would be.

Juan murmured into her ear, "Let me show you the bedroom." He took her hand and led her on a tour through the house. The master suite was larger than the lodge they now lived in, with a sitting area and a bathroom with a large jetted soaking tub and a shower. Everywhere they turned, there were windows.

Piper turned off the bedroom lights and looked out at the ocean and the ribbon of twinkling lights that stretched along the coastline in either direction. She sighed. "Is this real?"

"It's as real as our love that has survived against the odds, against opposition, and through separation."

Piper turned and pressed her body against his. "There's just one thing."

"What is it? We can fix it." He'd expected to make some adjustments here and there. As long as the overall plan pleased her, he could make it all work. He looked into her eyes, waiting to hear what was lacking.

"There's no bed."

"Oh, I think we can manage without one." He proceeded to show her just how.

LATER THAT EVENING, as they sat in a restaurant waiting for dinner, Piper held out her left hand beside the champagne flute and snapped an engagement-ring selfie. "This would be a lot easier if I were right-handed." But she managed and went on to compose and send the photo in a half-dozen separate text messages.

Juan leaned back, amused. "Wouldn't it be easier to just send a group text to your entire contact list?"

Piper looked at him with wonder, "Why didn't I think of that?"

Juan held out his palm. "I was kidding!"

She grinned. "I know. So am I. But I had to send one to my father and Lainey before I went public."

Juan lifted an eyebrow. "I'm sure they'll be thrilled."

"And to Avery."

"I'm surprised she hasn't run in here screaming."

Piper smiled. "And a few others in my inner circle of friends."

He reached over and took hold of her hand, grinning and moving the ring back and forth on her finger.

Piper eyed his amused grin. "Are you laughing at me for being so ridiculously happy?"

"Be as happy as you like. I am."

"You just hide it better than I do."

He leaned back, looking particularly handsome, and took a sip of champagne. "If it helps, on the inside, I'm doing an Irish step dance."

Piper laughed. "Oh, I'd like to see that."

"Sorry. I'm not taking any chances until after we've sealed the deal. Besides, we need to leave something for the wedding night."

"Oh, so it's naked step dancing. Now you've got my attention."

He studied her with a perturbed frown, but the upturned corner of his mouth betrayed him. "Seriously, Piper, you worry me sometimes. It's not gonna happen, you know."

"Aw, c'mon. Not even a little Scottish sword dance?"

"What, and slice up my toes?"

She rolled her eyes. "Okay. Just a few ballet leaps across the bedroom."

"You couldn't take it."

"It would take more than bad dancing to scare me away."

Juan looked offended. "Who said anything about bad? I was thinking of your health. The sight of my manly physique and my twinkling toes might be too much for your heart."

She gazed into his deep-brown eyes. "Well, I do love your manly physique." She was no longer kidding. But before she could expound on the topic, their dinner arrived.

PIPER HAD JUST PUT two slices of bread in the toaster when her phone dinged with yet another text from Avery. She smiled and texted her back while Juan got ready for work.

Before Juan started on the house, Piper took him to her parents' to share their good news in person over coffee. She had purposely sent them the engagement ring photos the previous night to cushion the blow for her father before they got together in person. When they arrived at the house, Hadley greeted Juan with a handshake and pat on the shoulder, which was the best-case scenario and a relief. Not that anything Hadley did would have gotten in the way of the wedding this time. Any disapproval would have been sadly noted but not heeded. She and Juan were adults now, and in control of their lives.

But the Hadley who met them this morning was a different man from the one who had laid down the law years ago. His improved attitude, even if it was just reluctant acceptance, pleased Piper. It was progress.

With Juan off to work, Piper went to the Dockside Café to meet Avery. There was some squealing over the engagement. But who could fault her best friend for being so happy for her? As they sipped their coffee and looked over the menu, it wasn't long before Grayson Endicott's name came up. Of course, that meant sharing the news of her arrest.

"Pipes! Why didn't you tell me? You should have called me!"

The engagement excitement had been fine, but Piper lowered her voice and looked at Avery with pleading eyes. "Shh. I'm telling you now. No one else knows, so let's keep it that way."

"Oh, absolutely." Avery nodded emphatically as the server arrived to take their order.

"Good to see you, Piper. Given up your life of crime, have you?" Her old high school classmate-turned-server was doing all she could to suppress a grin. "Small town. Word gets around."

Piper lifted her eyes. "It was a misunderstanding, that's all."

"Yeah. Word is, he misunderstood when you punched him in the face."

"I'll have a bowl of clam chowder." Without looking, Piper handed the menu back to the server.

Avery's eyes never left the menu. "I'll have the salad—extra cheese, extra croutons, and extra dressing on the side. Oh, and some bread, extra butter—not margarine, please." She lifted her eyes to the server and shrugged. "New diet."

When the server was out of earshot, Avery leaned closer. "So? What happened?"

Piper filled her in on the details of her ill-fated visit with Grayson. "Any news from your contacts?"

"Well, yes. I've been dying to tell you. But you had to go and get engaged, which completely back-burnered my news."

"What is it?"

Avery leaned on the table and spoke softly. "This really is a secret."

"And my arrest wasn't?"

"No, really, you can't tell a soul."

"Not even Juan?"

"Okay, Juan. No one else. Promise?"

"Promise."

Avery lifted her eyebrows and spoke in low tones. "Our friend G.E. is already under investigation by the SEC." Avery's eyes brightened as she gave Piper an affirming nod. "Apparently, he set up a company that manages hedge funds."

"The Endicott Group."

Avery smirked. "It's fake, just a mailing address and phone service at a virtual office. After that, all he needed was some letterhead and the trust of his friends."

Piper shook her head. "Like golf buddies."

Avery sighed. "He worked through friends, and then friends of friends. They all knew him. He was one of them, came from the right kind of family, went to the right schools, and belonged to the right clubs. Why wouldn't they trust him?

"But after a while, some of his New York investors began to complain, so he came up here to expand operations. So far, they've found over three dozen investors in his sketchy hedge fund. But they didn't know about the investors up here until they saw your father's file. So you've helped drive a nail in the coffin."

"When are they going to arrest him?"

"I don't know any more, just that they're building their case against him."

Piper slapped her palms to the table. "That's fantastic."

Avery's smile faded. "But you know, in these cases, the chance of recovering the money is..."

"Not good?"

"Snowball in hell."

Piper sighed. "Poor Daddy. Literally."

Avery's eyes warmed with sympathy. "But at least that bastard Grayson will get what he deserves."

"He deserves far more than he'll probably get." Piper scowled.

"Well, a punch in the face was a good start." Avery smiled.

Piper laughed. "I'd be happy to punch him again."

"Pipes, have you learned nothing from your life of crime?"

"Yeah, those chiseled features of his hurt my knuckles. But, like most criminals, my greatest regret is getting caught."

THIRTEEN

Piper's parents returned for a final walkthrough of the house before officially putting it on the market. Juan took them from one room to the other, pointing out all of his improvements—the repairs, fresh paint, and flooring. Outside, he'd done what he could in the middle of winter to maximize curb appeal. A recent coating of snow against the backdrop of the harbor left it looking so postcard perfect that Hadley's eyes looked a bit misty as he shook Juan's hand and thanked him. The real-estate agent had an open house scheduled for the following Sunday, which left one more pressing event until then.

Hadley, Lainey, and Juan came to the lodge to have coffee after the walkthrough. When everyone had a cup in their hand, Piper said, "There's no easy way to say this. I've been arrested. My preliminary hearing is tomorrow."

"What happened?" Lainey asked. "Are you all right?"

"I looked over your finances like I promised, and, well, Daddy, it looks like Grayson's a crook. Yes, Grayson, the right kind of man from the right kind of people, stole from you. When I figured it out, I was angry. So I went to talk to him, but I lost my temper and punched him."

Piper couldn't tell what upset her father more—that Piper had been arrested or that Grayson had turned out to be a not-so-great prospect, either for his investments or for his daughter. After he worked through what he'd heard, Hadley asked, "What will you do?"

Juan explained that he'd retained a criminal defense attorney. On a personal note, it would help Piper to have family there at the hearing as a show of support.

THE FOLLOWING MORNING, they walked through the metal detectors and went into the court-room, where they sat waiting for Piper's case to be called. Piper had been dreading this because it would mean seeing Grayson again. She worried about her father having to face him as well. But they waited and waited, and Grayson didn't show. When their case was announced, the prosecuting attorney asked her attorney to approach the bench. Next thing Piper knew, the case was dismissed.

They all left and gathered outside the courthouse.

Juan looked cautiously pleased as he turned to the lawyer. "So that's it? It's all over?"

He nodded. "That's it. The case is dismissed. You're free to get on with your life." He smiled at Piper.

"And I won't have a criminal record?"

"No," said her lawyer, with a satisfied smile.

Piper extended her hand. "Thank you. Thank you for everything."

"You're welcome."

As he shook hands with Juan and went on his way, Juan put his arm around Piper's shoulders. "The only bars in your future are the ones that serve drinks."

"Sounds good to me." She sank into his enveloping arms and sighed as the good news sank in.

THE IDEA SOUNDED SO GOOD, in fact, that Piper, Juan, and her parents were at a bar sharing a celebratory drink an hour later, when Piper's phone rang.

"There she is. She was supposed to be here by now." She pressed the button to answer her cell phone. "Avery, you've missed the first round of drinks, but if you hurry, I'm sure you can catch up."

Piper looked so stunned that the others stopped talking and stared, waiting to hear what had just made her blanch. She ended the call and turned her wide eyes to Juan. "They've issued a warrant. A friend of Avery's told her in confidence, so we're not supposed to know. But they're going to arrest him."

Hadley looked victorious. "He'll finally pay for the damage he's done. That's some consolation. I hope he rots in prison, the bastard." Lainey reached over and squeezed his hand.

It hurt Piper to see how the news had affected her father. For him, it was bittersweet news. Even though Grayson would pay for his crimes, Hadley would never recover his financial losses, and that had to weigh heavily on him.

FOURTEEN

Piper celebrated her legal victory the following day by packing, cleaning, and moving to Juan's new house. With her house on the market and people soon to be walking the property at all hours, it seemed like the right time to move. Juan's house was practically finished, so there was no real reason to stay.

Piper loaded the last box into her car, an assortment of items she'd needed until the end, such as coffee maker, computer, and her new high-resolution tablet she'd stood in line to buy on its first day in stores. Had she known she'd soon be losing her job, she wouldn't have bought it, but it was too late for regrets like that now. It beeped, so she opened the cover and checked her messages.

"You're addicted to that thing, you know." Juan looked at her as though she were a pitiful creature.

She looked at him with wide eyes. "I can stop any time."

"How 'bout now?"

Their eyes locked for a moment. Piper caved. With an eye roll and an even bigger sigh, she set it on top of the box and closed the back hatch of her car.

For a moment, they stood and looked back at the lodge. "I love our new home, but I'll miss this place. When I left Boston, I was sure my winter at the lodge would be my worst winter yet. But it's turned out to be my best."

Juan slipped an arm about her waist. "But we're beginning a new chapter together, and all that poetic stuff."

Piper couldn't tear her eyes from the lodge. "Maybe the new owner will rent the lodge out to us now and then."

Juan slowly turned and regarded her with a questioning frown. "I could have saved myself so much trouble and just built a hut for us."

"Oh, no, I didn't mean—what I meant was, well, there are memories here. The first time I knew there was something between us, you were standing right over there. I'd seen you around at school, but we'd never talked. There you were, and when you turned and looked right at me, I fell a little in love on the spot."

"Just a little?" He looked into her eyes with a knowing smile that made Piper's heart skip a beat.

She lifted her eyes and confessed. "Well, okay, a lot."

He slipped his hands through her hair and held her face. "We'll make new memories. And it's not like the old ones are going anywhere. We've got each other."

"You're right. Let's go make some."

"Memories or love?" Juan's eyes sparkled.

Piper gazed into his eyes. "Do I have to choose one?"

Juan touched his forehead to hers. "No, I never said that."

As he walked her to her car, Juan cursed.

"What?" Piper stood behind her open car door.

"Ugh. I just remembered I'm out of caulk. There's some trim that needs finishing up before the open house, and the hardware store closes in an hour. I'll tell you what. It's next door to the pizza place. Why don't I pick up a pie for dinner?"

Piper folded her arms on the top of the car door. "Perfect! It'll be our first dinner in our new home. I like the sound of that—home. While you're doing that, I'll get the wine started." She grinned at his disapproving smirk. "Just doing my part."

"Save some for me."

"Okay, but no drinking and caulking!"

Juan leaned closer and gave her that look that always made her knees buckle. "No, I'll save the caulking for the morning. I've got much better plans for tonight."

"Well, then. Sounds like a plan!" Piper got into her car, and the two headed in separate directions.

When Piper arrived at the house shrouded in fog and dusk, Juan's motion-sensor lighting turned on as she pulled into the driveway. She fumbled with her phone to unlock the door but accidentally unlocked everything. "Oh well, whatever. It's open," she muttered to herself. But as she leaned into the door, it locked, and she bumped her shoulder against it. As she fumbled with the security app, she found herself longing for an old-fashioned metal key to put into the lock. "Agh!" Just as she was eyeing the window with narrow eyes, the lock clicked, and she was in.

Her frustration faded as she looked around her new home and thought of her new life with Juan. Although they hadn't set a date, they'd talked about being married here in June, when the lupines were in bloom. She began daydreaming about an outdoor wedding as she pulled out two wineglasses and opened the bottle.

Her wedding. She'd never been one of those huge wedding types. She just wanted Juan. Close friends and family could come too, she supposed. She smiled to herself as she pulled two plates out of a moving box and washed them in the sink.

An arm clamped around her waist. "Juan, what the hell?" She knew as she said it, it couldn't be Juan. But some part of her brain denied this could even be happening. She struggled to free herself, but cold metal pressed into her neck.

"You've put me in kind of a bind."

It wasn't Juan's voice. But how could this be happening in her safe little town? Things like this happened in the city, not here. Panic spread through her chest, and she couldn't breathe for a moment. Her thoughts were as frenetic as her racing heartbeat.

Think, Piper. It was a male voice, and he sounded familiar, but she couldn't quite place it. Then her stomach sank. "Grayson. Look, I'm sorry I punched you, but a gun? C'mon, put that down. Let's just talk about this."

"I'd love to chat, but we've got to go." He gripped her arm and yanked her toward the door.

Piper tried to resist. If she could stall until Juan got home, it would be two against one—plus a gun.

Not great odds, but a better situation than hers, at the moment.

He stopped and pressed the gun barrel into her neck until her eyes teared from the pain. His voice was even and calm.

"Either walk to the car, or I'll shoot you. You're a smart girl. Make a smart choice."

She stopped struggling. He lowered the gun to her back and grabbed the car keys from the counter. "Where's your phone?"

"In my purse."

He dumped out the contents and put her phone in his pocket.

Once outside, he walked her to the passenger side and told her to get in. "Climb over to the other side. You're driving."

Grayson sat on the passenger side with his gun pointed at Piper. As directed, she pulled out of the driveway and headed down Main Street.

"Where are we going?"

"To the bank."

"Well, I hope you're not planning on getting money from my account. I am unemployed, after all. You'll be lucky if it's not overdrawn."

"No, you'll be lucky—because I need money, and it's your fault I can't get to mine."

"I don't know what you're talking about."

"Some feds came to my house, and they spoke with my housekeeper."

"And that's my fault?" Piper tried to sound calm, but she could hear the strained edge in her voice. She hoped that he wouldn't.

"They showed her their badges and asked all sorts of questions about me."

Piper drove through town, keeping an eye out for police cars. "You're still not making sense."

"Good try, Piper. But I happened to turn the corner and see their car there, so I followed them. They drove back to the federal building. Hard to say whether they were FBI, SEC, IRS, or some other set of initials. It doesn't really matter. What matters is, as those two were walking into the building, guess who showed up?"

"I don't know."

"Our friend, Avery. Turns out she knew them. Not only that, but they walked in together looking very chummy."

"You know, Grayson, this is all very interesting and has nothing to do with me."

"Yes, that's what I thought at first. Why would Avery be there?"

"Because she has friends?"

"Yeah, like you. You're a good friend of hers. And those friends of your friend came to my house asking about me and my business. Quite a coincidence. The thing is, I don't really believe in coincidences."

"Well, that's quite a collection of assumptions you've got there."

"Yeah, they probably wouldn't hold up in court, but since this isn't a court and I'm holding a gun, I don't really need proof, do I? I don't even care if you deny it. At this point, it doesn't matter. What matters is, I need some cash. I can't access my accounts without my movements being traced. So you're going to get me the cash that I need so I can get on with my life."

"I would love to do that, but I've already told you I don't have that kind of money."

"But your boyfriend does."

"I don't know what makes you think he has money."

"Well, I have to admit, I was surprised. There I was at the winter carnival looking through the list of donors. I make a habit of it. Lists like that are a great way to find future investors. And whose name should I find there but Juan's?"

"He's a good person."

Grayson nodded. "Yeah. If he weren't such a good person with such a large amount of money to donate, you wouldn't be here right now. Sometimes life's just so goddamn ironic."

Grayson smiled. "Ten thousand dollars for a local festival? That's quite a donation."

"He loves his community."

"Let's hope he loves you even more. We're about to put that to the test. Pull in here." Grayson pointed to a store parking lot. "Drive around to the back."

When she had parked the car, Grayson said, "Listen and follow directions, or I might have to use this." He pointed his gun at her. "In a few minutes, I'm going to hand you your phone, and you're going to call Juan. You will read exactly what's on this paper I'm holding. If you say even one extra word, I'll pull this trigger. Do you understand?"

"Yes." Piper's hands trembled as she took the paper from him.

Grayson reached into his pocket and pulled out her phone. "Set it on speakerphone and make the call."

Piper dialed Juan's number.

"Piper! Where are you? I got home, and the car was gone. Your purse is spilled out on the counter. I was worried about you."

Piper read, "Someone's pointing a gun at my head."

"What? Piper! Where are you?"

Hearing Juan's voice set her emotions careening out of control. Grayson pushed the gun barrel into her neck. Her voice wavered. "If you want to see me alive, get a cash advance from every card that you own, and withdraw the full limit you can from your bank. I'll call back in twenty minutes. Have the money ready. No police, or he'll shoot me."

Grayson grabbed the phone and threw it into a nearby trash receptacle. "Good girl. Now drive."

He sent her down back roads where no one would see them. After making a few turns, they went down a private dirt road. Grayson seemed to know where he was going. He'd obviously planned it. They hadn't passed a house in over a mile. Grayson told her to stop at the end of the road.

"Now we wait." Grayson seemed oddly relaxed. She supposed stealing from friends and acquaintances made a person that way, as if he were immune to consequences suffered by ordinary people. Grayson looked at his watch. "It's a shame bank machines limit withdrawals, but this should get me where I need to go."

"And where's that?"

Grayson chuckled. "Do you really think I'd tell you?"

"Well, good luck with the amount you're going to get out of us. I've never seen Juan pull out more than one credit card."

"Oh, he'll manage. Because if I don't leave with

at least twenty-five thousand, well... let's just say he'll be motivated to find it somehow."

"You didn't tell him an amount."

Grayson shrugged. "He might come up with more. Why limit our options? Everything's negotiable, and the side that's emotional always loses."

Piper didn't press further. She didn't know what Grayson was capable of, but his sangfroid disturbed her. While they waited, to keep herself from panicking, she let her mind race through the possible scenarios for how this could play out.

As she saw it, the best case would be if Grayson just wanted enough cash to implement his exit strategy. He had to have one. No one could continue to rob Peter to pay Paul without knowing it would eventually catch up with him. He had to have known that a day would come when he'd have to escape his investors, as well as the law. He probably had offshore accounts or maybe even a numbered Swiss bank account at the ready. She was surprised he hadn't had cash on hand, packed away in a go bag. Maybe he'd depleted all his reserves. Regardless, he would need to escape—probably to a country with no extradition treaty. She had no idea where that might be. She supposed Cuba was closest. Even with a fake passport, he could get passage on a boat to escape undetected. From there, there were probably dozens of countries where he could go and disappear.

But why risk a kidnapping? There were too many moving parts to this plan. He was no fool. He had to have seen what a risk he was taking. He must have been desperate for cash.

The next scenario that came to mind involved revenge, with the above escape plan to follow. If he truly thought she'd turned him in, which made perfect sense since she more or less had, then he might want to make her pay. In that case, this was not going to be a mere kidnapping. Once he got his money, he might never release her. If her life was in danger, she needed to focus her thoughts on escaping. She might only get one chance, so she would have to think fast and be ready to flee.

FIFTEEN

Driving with a pizza box and caulk tube on the passenger seat beside him, Juan was nearly home. He thought he saw Piper's car pass him, heading in the other direction. He looked back, but it was too dark to see who was driving. She drove an all-wheel-drive compact that was common in the region. Its silver color was even more common, so Juan decided he'd just seen a car like hers. But when he got home and found her car gone and the house unlocked, something seemed off. She might have run out to the store for some item misplaced in a packing box somewhere. But inside, he found her purse contents strewn over the counter. Then the phone rang, and everything changed.

He hung up from the call and considered Grayson's warning not to tell the police, but with

Piper involved, he had to think of what was best for her. If he tried to handle this himself, as instructed, they'd be entirely at Grayson's mercy. Juan would do anything for Piper, but if he tried to play hero and something went wrong, it could cost Piper her life. He wasn't prepared for that risk. At least with the police involved, they brought training and resources that could save Piper's life.

On his way to the station, Juan called the police. He gave them Piper's cell number to see if they could track her location. He told them he didn't want police cars seen anywhere near the house in case Grayson was watching. On the way, he called Avery and asked her to contact the people she knew who'd been planning Grayson's arrest. With all of the resources he could think of on the same page, they'd have to find Piper and bring her home safely. There was no other option.

A half hour later, an officer radioed in. They'd found Piper's phone in a trash receptacle. It had Grayson's fingerprints all over it—proof to back up Juan's insistence that it was Grayson who'd kidnapped her. Given the time of the call and how fast they could travel, they had to be within a twenty-mile radius. Knowing these things felt like progress, and yet Piper wasn't any safer.

By the time he arrived at the station, the police

had contacted the town's only taxi company, who had taken a fare to Juan's address. So the two were in Piper's car, but they still had no idea where she and Grayson were. Knowing it was a twenty-mile or so radius wasn't enough.

PIPER SAT in the driver's seat staring straight ahead while Grayson kept his eyes and his gun pointed on her. Her car was a hatchback, so it wasn't as though he could have locked her in the trunk. He could have tied her up, though. But then, if he were pulled over, it would be hard to explain a woman tied up in the back. And she might have managed to attack him from behind. For whatever reason, being in the driver's seat gave her an advantage he either hadn't thought of or had assumed his gun would offset. If an opportune moment arose, she could open the door and make a run for it. She could even engage the car's child-safety locks, so he'd have to climb over the gearshift to get to the driver's side door to get out.

He seemed to prefer having her do the speaking on their phone calls. She couldn't imagine trying to mask his identity would do him any good at this point. There was too much evidence pointing to him. But he might need proof of life, which her voice on the phone calls provided. So he needed her alive—at least for the next call. And he needed the money, so he wouldn't harm her yet. That gave her a slight sense of safety, for now, which was good.

Making a run here in the woods presented too many dangerous variables. Of course, no matter where she made her escape, he could shoot her. But if that happened here, she'd be helpless. Even if she managed to get far enough away to hide from him, she could pass out and never be found. If she got away without being shot, she might fall in a rut or fall off the edge of a steep hill. With her fear of heights, that scenario would not play out well. If she could hold on until they were back on more well-traveled roads, she could make her move then and have a chance of finding help and making it to safety.

"I have to pee."

Piper turned and scowled. "You're just classy every step of the way, aren't you?"

"Hey, the bladder wants what the bladder wants." He opened the door and stood outside the car with one hand on the gun while he managed to unzip his fly.

Piper turned away in disgust.

When he was finished, he got back in the car and pulled out his phone. "Start driving."

He touched the button and waited for his phone to turn on. "What's Juan's number?"

Piper told him, and Grayson dictated a text message into his phone. "Put the money in a backpack. Be ready at midnight. I'll call with instructions." He pressed Send, then turned off the phone. "Turn left here."

"You sent him a text?"

"You have a problem with that?"

"What if he doesn't get it? What if his phone is dead? What if there's no signal?"

"You're a real negative Nancy, aren't you? Turn right up here."

She didn't think the police would be able to track Grayson's phone if it was turned off, so Piper tried to come up with a reason to turn it back on. "Shouldn't you check to make sure that he got it?"

Grayson smiled. "You're so cute when you're trying to be clever. Trust me, Romeo got the message."

AN OLD ICE cream stand lay at the bottom of a long hill. There, beside the building, shaded by trees, they waited.

"An hour from now? Wouldn't you rather get it

over with?"

"What, you've got someplace to go?"

"Yes, as a matter of fact."

Piper looked down at the road. Cars came by now and then, but not often enough to rely on someone helping her. She couldn't trust that Grayson was just in it for the money and count on him setting her free after getting the ransom. He'd used his own phone to send the text, so he had to know that there would be evidence connecting him to her kidnapping, even without Piper to testify.

Then her heart sank. She had no way of knowing if this was really his phone or if it was just a burner phone that he'd throw away after he'd gotten the money. So there still might not be enough evidence connecting him to this. Not having her as a witness would serve as insurance in case they arrested him.

They'd still have him for securities fraud, but he might get away with the kidnapping. She still found it hard to believe he would shoot her, and yet, as she looked at that gun barrel, it was just as hard to be sure that he wouldn't.

Grayson had told Juan not to involve the police. But, knowing Juan, he had more faith in them than in Grayson's word, so he probably went straight to them. If they showed up, Grayson might panic and do something desperate—like shoot her.

This might be her best time to escape.

JUAN SAT at a table in the precinct. The FBI was there by the time Grayson's text message came in.

An agent spoke without looking up from his laptop. "Have you ever seen his phone? What brand is it?"

When Juan told him, the agent shook his head. "That brand with a text? Virtually impossible. He probably texted and then turned it off. He must have disabled his 2G, 'cause I'm getting nothing. I can try to locate the towers it last pinged, but I won't get a specific enough location. Right now, all we can tell is that he's somewhere within a twenty-mile radius."

Thirty minutes went by. Juan got up and paced. "Can't we do anything?"

"With no leads, it's a waiting game now."

Juan wanted to go outside and yell or run off his anger, but he couldn't leave in case something happened. He thought through every move she would have made from the time they parted back at the lodge. They'd loaded her car, and she'd gone to the house. How had Grayson managed to abduct her? There were no signs of breaking in, and yet, knowing Piper, she wouldn't have opened the door to him. If she hadn't flatly refused to speak with him, she might just as easily have pretended that she wasn't home. And yet, her purse contents were dumped out on the counter, so somehow he got in, and he took her away.

Hadley and Lainey rushed into the station. The FBI agent briefed them and questioned them to see if they knew anything that might help. They hadn't heard from Grayson. Why would they? He'd avoided them as soon as they began asking questions about their money.

Hadley prattled nervously to Lainey. "I never thought he'd be capable of this. It just doesn't make sense. He comes from a good family with money. We have friends in common. We've played golf together." Lainey squeezed his hand.

Juan walked away and looked out the window, all the while clenching and releasing his fists. If Grayson hurt Piper, he'd need protection, because right now Juan was ready to kill him.

"I'VE GOTTA GO." Piper squirmed in the car seat.

"What?"

"I've got to go to the bathroom."

He made an exasperated sound.

"What? You went. It's been hours."

He thought for a moment. "Okay. Just squat outside the door there." He pointed with his gun and then pointed it at her.

She ran her fingertips along the armrest until they got to the lock, then she pressed it as she pushed open the door and pushed the gear shift into neutral. The car started to move. Piper dropped to the ground as Grayson fired a shot. The car rolled downhill slowly as Grayson pushed against his locked door. He tried to push the gear shift into Park, but it slipped out of gear. He struggled to get his long legs over the console and position himself in the driver's side. Once there, he pulled the emergency brake as the car struck a tree, and the airbag deployed.

No more than a half minute later, Grayson stumbled out of the car and ran up the hill toward Piper. He hadn't fired his gun, but she couldn't assume he didn't have it, so she headed for the woods and kept running parallel to the road. A car came around the bend. Piper ran to the road and flagged it down. The door opened. Someone pulled her inside and closed the door. "Piper Harriman?"

"Yes."

"FBI. You're safe now."

They sat in the car as two other vehicles approached Grayson from opposite directions. They stopped, opened their doors, and crouched behind them. "FBI, Grayson Endicott. Drop your gun! Get on the ground!"

Grayson complied and lay on the ground as an officer searched and then cuffed him.

As they put him into a car, a police patrol car arrived, and Juan got out. Piper rushed to him, and he held her.

Piper clung to him. "I don't know how they found me, but they did, and you're here."

Juan kissed her forehead and hair and clutched her to him. "It was that tablet of yours."

Piper gave him a questioning look.

Juan nodded. "In the box in your car. I kept thinking about what happened, trying to figure out how Grayson had gotten to you. I finally remembered that tablet."

Piper's eyes widened. "It has GPS tracking software to find it if it's been stolen or lost."

Juan shook his head with wonder. "I love that damn tablet." He looked into her eyes and took her face in his hands. "And I love you."

Their kiss was interrupted by an FBI agent. "Are you two ready to go?"

Piper nodded and looked at Juan. "I'm ready to go home." They walked arm in arm to a waiting FBI car.

SIXTEEN

The Harriman house sold quickly. They got the news the next morning, to everyone's surprise and to Hadley and Lainey's mixed feelings. They'd needed to sell it for the money, but their sadness at losing it was apparent. It had been home for Hadley's whole life.

Hadley stood alone by the gate that led down to the dock and looked out at the view of the ocean. Piper joined him and silently slipped her hand into his. He'd announced the news over lunch, and they'd come back home for a bittersweet celebration—all except Juan, who'd had an errand to run on the way. Lainey made her way down the stone walkway and joined Hadley and Piper.

"There are a lot of memories here." Hadley looked down and swallowed.

Lainey said, "We've got a few weeks until clos-ing. Plenty of time to get sentimental."

Piper turned to hide her eye roll. For her, Lainey was still an outsider who would never understand. She hadn't grown up on the land of her ancestors. This was more than a building or land. It was her heritage and her father's and grandfather's.

Juan arrived and joined them. "It's going to be okay."

Hadley looked at Juan as though he were too young to understand things like memories and family.

Juan spoke plainly. "I bought it."

Three stunned faces stared at him.

"I've just met with a lawyer. I know what this place means to your family. Your parents and their parents raised families here. I want Piper's children, our children, to know this as home. I want them to grow up spending time with their grandparents here." He looked at Hadley. "I'm having a lawyer draw up some papers. After closing, the property will be in a revocable trust, yours and Lainey's to live in for the rest of your lives, after which, it will go to your grandchildren." He looked at Piper and smiled softly. "Our children."

Piper hastened to add, "If and when! Calm down, everybody. There are no children yet. None on the way!" She looked at Juan and said softly, "Yet."

WHEN THEY GOT HOME that evening, Piper slipped her arms about Juan's waist. "You are full of surprises."

He grinned. "There's one more." He took her hand and led her to a room on the first floor that she'd never been in. The door had been covered with plastic construction sheeting while workers completed the house. Now the sheeting was gone.

Several steps from the door, Piper stopped, and her face wrinkled up. "Oh... this isn't going to be some sort of, uh, you know... playroom, is it?"

Juan's face went blank.

Piper started to ramble. "I mean, not that there's anything wrong with it. Consenting adults, and all that. But, it's not really my thing."

"Piper, stop." He shut his eyes and heaved a sigh. He pulled a key out of his pocket, which she eyed with suspicion. He opened the door.

She glanced up at him and tentatively walked to the doorway and looked inside. Her apprehension was replaced with confusion. "It's an office."

"For you."

She gazed at him, puzzled.

Juan shrugged. "I know how much it's bothered you to be out of work. So I thought, tax season is coming. You could work for yourself—here at home. I've added a door to the driveway for your clients."

She looked at him with eyes shining and laughed. "It's perfect! I wasn't expecting this."

With an amused smirk, he said, "I could tell."

Piper threw her arms about Juan's neck. "You get me. I love you for that!"

SEVENTEEN

The lupines were in bloom the following summer. In rippling plumes of pastel, they sloped down to the water, where wind puffed out the sails of the boats in the harbor as they headed to sea. Two dozen guests milled about on the lawn of the Harriman house on this perfect June day. As a string quartet played, the guests made their way to their seats.

Avery walked out of the back door on the arm of the handsome Nurse Noah and proceeded down the grass aisle between the white wooden chairs. On Hadley's arm, Piper followed, wearing a flowing white linen ankle-length dress. Juan stood waiting for her in a suit and a tie, looking tall, dark, and manly, with his muscles confined to a well-tailored suit. Their eyes met. After long years apart, they were finally together. This time it would be for a lifetime.

THANK YOU!

Thank you, reader. With so many options, I appreciate your choosing my book to read. Your opinion matters, so please consider sharing a review to help other readers.

BOOK NEWS

Would you like to know when the next book comes out? Click below to sign up for the J.L. Jarvis Journal and get book news, free books, and exclusive content delivered monthly.

news.jljarvis.com

ACKNOWLEDGMENTS

Editing by Red Adept Editing
redadeptediting.com

ABOUT THE AUTHOR

J.L. Jarvis is a left-handed former opera singer/teacher/lawyer who writes books. She now lives and writes on a mountaintop in upstate New York.

jljarvis.com

facebook.com/jljarvis1writer

twitter.com/JLJarvis_writer

instagram.com/jljarvis.writer

bookbub.com/authors/j-l-jarvis

pinterest.com/jljarviswriter

goodreads.com/5106618.J_L_Jarvis

amazon.com/author/B005G0M2Z0

youtube.com/UC7kodjlaG-VcSZWhuYUUl_Q